When Grandpa Was Little Eddie

Tales from an
Appalachian Boyhood

By

Ed Somerville

WWW.OAKLEAPRESS.COM

Dedication

This book is dedicated to my mother, of course.

Mom loved "getting into mischief", and she hated to see children sitting around bored. She had a "hands off" approach to parenting and allowed her six boys to experience life to the fullest. She discouraged watching television and encouraged creativity. She was a writer and a musician. She lived big.

She always wanted to be a missionary, but settled for a mission field of six sons. Today, those boys are grown. Among them are PhD's, a lawyer, a businessman, a psychologist, a senior pastor, a missions pastor, a missionary, educators, entrepreneurs, musicians, artists, poets, husbands and fathers. She's leaving quite a legacy!

It is also dedicated to my grandchildren.

These days many children live boring lives. Dreams are small, passions tepid, imagination crippled. Kids get lost in cyberspace. Because of real and imagined danger, families live as if they were under siege. Children's safety is purchased at the price of a lukewarm existence.

This country and God's kingdom are looking for future leaders. We are in need of young people with courage and creativity who are passionate and daring.

The world needs youth with big dreams; youngsters that can get knocked down and keep going, kids not afraid to try hard things. We are desperate for a generation that can live large, laugh long and love hard.

As a grandfather I pray for my grandchildren and want the best for them. My life has not always been easy, but it has been fun and lived to the fullest. I dedicate these stories of growing up with five brothers in the hills of Appalachia to my grandchildren and others like them. I hope some of these stories will be inspirational. I beg forgiveness for the rest!

"Granddaddy"
Ed Somerville

Contents

Preface

The Appalachian Mountains are some of the oldest in the world. Their gentle ridges run for 1,500 miles, paralleling the eastern seaboard of the United States. These rolling green hills, crowned with dark, scented balsams and robed in magenta rhododendrons are home to deer, turkey and bear. They were also home to the Cherokee, Shawnee, and Mingo before the Europeans arrived. Early colonists flowed across the Piedmont until they washed up against the wall of the Blue Ridge and Allegheny Mountains, subsections of the larger Appalachian chain.

In the 1600's, while Tidewater society was planting cotton and building plantation houses, another group of restless adventurers was leaving the highlands of Scotland in search of a better life. Their children and grandchildren spent a century in Ireland and then pushed on to America in the 1700's. These Protestant immigrants came to be known as the "Scotch-Irish". They were resourceful and rugged, poets and warriors. When they found no room in the Piedmont, they headed for the hills of Appalachia, which may have reminded them of their old home in the Scottish highlands. In the 1800's, civilization pushed on beyond the Appalachians, but the ruggedness of the region created pockets of isolation where the pioneer spirit lived on. At the same time, the lack of infrastructure and industry left Appalachia at a definite disadvantage.

By the 1900's, the region was languishing. Coal operators moved into the area, but profits stayed with the big companies. Miners lived in shacks wedged between the river and the railroad tracks. In 1964, President Lyndon Johnson declared a "War on Poverty" in his State of the Union address. One of the principle battlefields was Appalachia.

My father, Jim Somerville, was a crusader. As a young Presbyterian pastor, he confronted racism and bigotry in the Deep South. One morning in 1960 he stepped out of the house to fetch the paper. There on the lawn were the ashes of a cross burned by the Ku Klux Klan. His legendary comment on stepping back inside: "It sure was a small one wasn't it?"
Unfortunately, the members of his congregation didn't see eye to eye with their pastor and suggested he search for another flock. He moved the family to the coalfields of Appalachia. In the South, he'd been convinced that black people were still people. In Appalachia, he grew to feel the same way about the poor. When President Johnson declared his war on poverty, my father was one of the first to enlist.

So it was that my brothers and I found ourselves growing up in a "holler" in West Virginia, in a falling-down house without indoor plumbing. We climbed the hills, skinny-dipped in the river, caught 'possums and ate snakes. What we lacked in money, we made up for in adventure. No one could have convinced us we were disadvantaged.

These stories are the result of that wonderful blend of five, active brothers, a pair of wise, loving parents, and the unlimited opportunities of the great outdoors. By the grace of God Little Eddie survived to record his adventures.

Chapter One
Wise, Virginia, 1960-67, Age 4-10

Ambushed by Goats

In the "toe" of Virginia lies the little town of Wise. Just to the west is the Cumberland Gap where pioneers had passed into the "dark and bloody ground of Kentucky." To the north is the Tug Fork of the Big Sandy River, the passionate battlefield of the Hatfields and McCoys. This was Carter family country, where the sounds of banjo and mandolin would set feet tapping to "Old Time" music. In 1960, Eddie's father had been run off from his pastorate in southern Alabama for thinking black people were human. As he settled his family into the parsonage at Wise, he had little idea he would again run into deep prejudice, this time against the poor, or that his ministry would eventually lead him to one of the most poverty-wracked areas in Appalachia.

Little Eddie and his younger brothers, Scotty and Jimmy, were blissfully ignorant of the heartache of the grownup world. They watched their dad untie the doghouse from the top of their old Ford and remove the board over the door. Lady, their black-and white rat terrier raced around the grass of her new home followed by four puppies that had enjoyed an air-conditioned ride on the roof all the way from Alabama.

Little Eddie wanted to see the mountains. The idea of vertical dirt fascinated him. He was thinking how fun it would be to get a shovel and start digging into the side of a mountain. In no time, you could make a little cave. Why, if you kept digging, you could make a whole house!

The boys explored their new residence. Across the front of the house was an impressive row of ancient spruce trees, their lower branches inviting the boys upward to adventure. In the back was a large, screened porch where the occasional sparrow got trapped. Forsythia bushes bloomed profusely, attracting thirsty honey bees. The boys enjoyed the challenge of catching the bees in Mason jars, just to see if they could do it without getting stung. Beds of the most exotic irises sprung up around the old brick foundations.

Inside the old house, the boys wandered through the big living room, stopping to admire the brick fireplace. They poked their heads into their parents' bedroom, then they rounded the corner to the kitchen. Instead of passing to the dining room, they turned right, up the narrow stairs that led to the second floor bedrooms. One, two, three...one for each of them! Little Eddie wasn't sure he wanted his own room; he preferred snuggling up to his brothers, but they objected because he often wet the bed.

When it was time for Little Eddie to go to school he didn't go to kindergarten. In fact, during first grade he only attended half days because there were too many kids and not enough teachers. The old elementary building had high windows and dark wooden floors the janitor cleaned with green sweeping compound. The bathrooms were in the basement, and bad little boys would stand at the ends of the long urinal trough, competing to see who could pee all the way across. Little Eddie's first grade teacher was an ancient lady named Miss Cherry. She had snowy white hair and always smelled a bit like sauerkraut. She'd taught generations of first graders and ran a tight ship. As a reward, she promised to give each child a sucker on the day they could count to a hundred. Little Eddie worked hard and was so proud the day he got his sucker. It was so much fun he asked his mom to buy some suckers. At home, he pretended to be the teacher and Scotty and Jimmy were his students. He drilled and drilled them until one day he proudly presented them with their own suckers. He took all the credit for their subsequent academic success!

His school was a long way from their house, almost a mile along a dirt road that wound through the country. It might seem strange today, but in those days kids walked to school, even little six-year-olds, even if it was a mile away, even if it was snowing, even if a herd of goats was wandering along the road! He remembers the afternoon he was walking slowly towards home when he suddenly heard the faint sound of bells in the distance. He turned around and looked behind him. There, coming around a bend, was a herd of about a dozen goats. The one in front had horns that looked huge to six-year-old Eddie. He picked up his pace, but the goats were gaining on him! What to do? In desperation, he left the road and climbed the steep bank to the woods above. He found a large tree and hunkered down behind it. Then he prayed!

Fortunately, the goats weren't worried about a trembling little first grader. They trotted right past, on their way to who knows where. He slid weakly down the bank and staggered home, glad to be alive.

Hell practice

Little Eddie's brothers were getting bigger and he found new ways to have fun with them. One way was a game he invented called "Hell Practice." He wanted to make sure his brothers didn't grow up to be sissies. They had to be toughened up. So he waited for the hottest day of the summer and dragged the old family sleeping bag out to the back yard. It was big, bulky, and brown. Then, to show them how to play, he crawled head first to the bottom of the bag and told them to sit on the opening. Sweat began to trickle down his back. Down his front. Into his eyes. Then it got hard to breathe. He grew afraid that he would suffocate!

"Let me out!" he yelled. His little brothers heard something that sounded like, "Leff be cow!"

"What? What did you say? What cow?"

The sweat was running down Little Eddie's underpants. "I said, 'Let me OUT!'"

"No, we don't see any cows. What do you want?" They stood up and opened the mouth of the sleeping bag. Eddie's sweaty toes poked out, and they grabbed him by the ankles. Heaving with all their might, they pulled him from the sleeping bag. He flopped on the grass like a dying fish. His eyes bulged. His skin was pale. He gasped for air.

"Boys," he said, "If that's what Hell is like...I don't wanna go!" They went off in search of something else to do.

The New Bike

Eddie and his brothers got an allowance each week. Five whole cents. But a nickel went further back in those days, and most Saturdays they would go to the Five and Dime store and spend their money on a bag of candy. The best deal was the gelatin orange slices with sugar coating. Once Eddie bought a Superball, a new invention that bounced like crazy!

Another time he spent his birthday money on a shiny change purse. He'd had his eye on the little blond girl in his class for some time and wanted to get her a present. To be honest, he'd had his eye on TWO little blond girls, and from one week to the next he would take turns bringing them candy. He just couldn't make up his mind which one would receive the purse! Each afternoon, before going home from school, Miss Cherry would dismiss the children row by row to go into the coat closet and gather their things. Eddie waited for his chance, and when he and one of the little blond girls were both in the closet, he pulled out the gift he'd carefully wrapped and presented it to her. Her eyes got big and she opened her mouth to shriek with delight. Eddie quickly put his hand over her mouth and whispered fiercely, "Shhhh! This is our secret. You can't tell anybody. Not Miss Cherry. Especially NOT any of the other girls.

When he dropped his hand, the little girl immediately ran out of the coat closet and straight to Miss Cherry's desk. Waving the gift over her head and looking around the room triumphantly, she declared, "Miss Cherry, look what Little Eddie gave me!!"

Little Eddie wanted to hide in the coat closet for the rest of his life.

He made up his mind that he was through with women. He had a new plan. If he and his brothers diligently saved their nickels each week they'd have enough to buy a bicycle in only one year! Eddie wasn't too worried about the fact that his little brothers' legs weren't long enough to reach the pedals. They'd grow.

To speed the process up, he and his brothers would walk along the side of the road and collect glass pop bottles. When they turned them in at the store, they were given a penny a piece! When birthdays rolled around, there was considerable pressure to donate birthday money to the bike fund.

At long last, the boys collected $34.95, the full amount, and mailed a check off to the Sears Roebuck Company. The days dragged by like molasses until one day a large rectangular box was delivered to the front door. The bike had come!

With some help from their dad, the bike was assembled. It was a thing of beauty with glistening red paint and mirror-like chrome. The sprocket chain was lubed with an exotic smelling oil. The rubber tires, their tread having never touched pavement, inspired awe. The boys rolled the bike out the door and onto the grass. At that moment it occurred to them; none of them knew how to ride a bike! Being the oldest, Eddie reasoned he should get the first chance. While his dad held the bike steady, Eddie climbed aboard and hollered, "Let her go!" His dad gave him a great push and he sailed majestically across the yard...for ten feet. Then his momentum ran out and the bike keeled over in the hydrangea bush. From somewhere deep underneath the foliage, Little Eddie paused to give thanks hydrangeas didn't have thorns! His brothers wandered over and peered into the bush. "Eddie, you O.K?" Eddie didn't answer.

Eating Yellow Jackets

In time, Eddie's next two brothers were born, Greg and Gray. Although they weren't twins, they could've been. One was born practically on the heels of the other. Now that there were seven people the family, they had to look for more economical ways to entertain themselves.

Dad had been a Boy Scout leader when his sons were very young. He used to teach his scouts to live off the land and impress them by eating granddaddy longlegs! Since the family couldn't afford Disney Land, their dad would take them camping. Every summer, he would pack up the old tent, plan a menu, load the car, and head to a national park. One place in particular was called Carolina Hemlocks. It was alongside a crystal-clear mountain creek that was just a little too cold to swim in, even for a bunch of burr-headed boys. It was bordered by towering hemlock trees whose feathery branches whispered in the night wind. Those were some wonderful times! The family would sit around the fire at night, Eddie's dad whittling a piece of red cedar, and listen to him tell stories. He had a regular character, Old Herbert Rabbit, who vaguely resembled himself and was a bit of a rascal that was always getting into a jam.

One morning Eddie and the boys emerged from their sleeping bags and crawled out of the tent, hungry as little bears. Their dad hunkered over the campfire, turning scrambled eggs in a camp skillet. While the boys waited, he suggested they toast a piece of bread. That was great fun, but what to put on it? He pointed them in the direction of the jelly jar. Unfortunately, SOMEONE (probably Little Eddie or one of his brothers) had left the lid off the jar all night. The jar was full of yellow jackets, an ornery yellow and black wasp. Most of them had drowned in the grape jelly, but not all.

"Ewww!" yelled Eddie.

"Disgusting!" agreed his little brothers.

"What?" came the voice of their dad. "What's wrong?"

"This jelly is full of bees!"

"What's wrong with that?" asked their father. "Probably full of protein!" And with that he picked up a piece of toast, slathered it with yellow jacket jelly, and took a big bite. He smiled and chewed with relish. He swallowed, and then he took another bite.

"Not a thing wrong with that," he declared, and left his boys staring after him. Jaws dropped, eyes bugged. Maybe their father was right, but no one hurried to try the new delicacy.

Gators, Ratty, and the Killer Chicken

When Little Eddie was in the third grade, he saw an advertisement in the back of a Marvel Comic book for a pet alligator. No kidding! You sent in five dollars, and in a couple of weeks a box from Florida would arrive at your mailbox with an honest to goodness baby alligator inside! It sounded too good to be true.

So Eddie saved up his allowance and collected more pop bottles. He cut the coupon out of the back of the comic book and carefully filled in his address. He folded a five dollar bill and inserted it into the envelope and dropped it in the mailbox. Then began the long vigil, anxiously checking the mailbox every afternoon when he got home from school. At long last, there was a cardboard box waiting for him with a return address in Florida!

He took the box to the kitchen and fished around in a drawer for his mom's wooden-handled, serrated breadknife. Carefully, he slid its edge under the tape and made an incision. Finally, he was able to open the box...just a crack. He put his eye up to the slit and peered into the box. GREAT BALLS of FIRE! To a little boy, it looked like they'd sent him a half-grown dinosaur! This gator may have been a baby at one point in time, but it had grown a lot since then. What would he feed it? Steaks? Suckling pigs? The neighborhood dogs?

As it turned out, he didn't have to worry about feeding it for more than a few weeks. One night, it mysteriously climbed out of it's cage, most likely intent on climbing the stairs to eat Little Eddie. On the way, however, it slipped into a gaping crack in the concrete slab of the back porch. In its thrashing, it got its neck twisted and when Little Eddie discovered it the next morning, it was stone, cold dead. Eddie was a little sad, and a little relieved. After all, what business did he have owning an animal that could've eaten him?

Little Eddie still wanted some kind of pet. One day he brought home a small white rat from his friend's house. She had white fur and pink eyes. Her tiny nose would twitch and her long white whiskers wiggled. Her small pink paws would hold food while she nibbled it. She would then lick her paws and wash her whole body frequently to keep clean. The only thing about her that was disgusting was her long, scaly rat tail. But, poor thing, she couldn't help it!

Little Eddie decided to name her "Ratty." He thought the name fit her well. Eddie fell in love with Ratty. She would run around on his blankets and hide in the tunnels he would make for her. She would take bits of dog food from his hand and sit up to eat them. She would snuggle into the soft place behind his ear when she rode on his shoulder. She hid in his pocket when he walked around the house.

One day, Little Eddie decided to make a parachute for Ratty. He found a cylindrical Quaker Oats box and lined it with soft rags. Then he punched four holes around the top edge. He tied one end of a string to the hole and the other end to the corner of a bed sheet. When all four corners of the sheet were tied to the strings, Little Eddie put Ratty into the box. Then he carried her upstairs and opened the window. Scotty and Jimmy waited down below with their arms outstretched.

On the first try, Little Eddie threw Ratty out the window, but the bed sheet got tangled. Ratty plunged toward the ground, but at the last minute she hit Scotty in the face. Not so good for Scotty but a lifesaver for Ratty! The boys looked her over and asked if she wanted to try again. She looked at them intently with her pink eyes and twitched her whiskers. They took that to mean "yes."

On the second try, Little Eddie made sure the bed sheet was all the way out the window and ready to spread in the air. He counted, "One. Two. Three..." and pitched her out. This time, the parachute worked perfectly and Ratty sailed gently down to the ground.

When the boy's asked her if she wanted to go again, there was a different look in her pink eyes, a sort of pleading look. Eddie thought he saw a tear. They decided she'd had all the fun she wanted for that day.

The next week, Little Eddie took her out exploring in the cow pasture beside their house. It was overgrown with tall grass and flowers. Eddie thought it would be like a jungle for Ratty. He let her down and she began to sniff the flowers and nibble the grass. He turned his head for a minute, and when he looked back, Ratty was gone! She'd scurried down a tunnel under the grass and was nowhere to be found. Little Eddie panicked. He pulled up tufts of grass and dug through the weeds, but Ratty was gone! After ten minutes of searching, Little Eddie sat down in the grass and cried.

He cried the next day. And the next. After a week had gone by, he opened the door to the basement stairs where Ratty's cage sat on its shelf. It looked so empty. He picked it up and carried it to the garage. It wouldn't be needed anymore. He cried again.

Several days later, Little Eddie wanted to play soccer in the backyard. His ball was down in the basement. He ran to get it, pulling open the door and racing down the steps. Something caught the corner of his eye. He stopped and walked back up the stairs. There on the shelf where the cage had been sat Ratty! Dirty, fat, and with a very pleased look on her little face. Little Eddie scooped her up and hugged her so hard her pink eyes bugged out. He ran for her cage and gave her fresh water and food. In return, a week later Ratty gave Little Eddie six pink babies. When they grew up, they were a beautiful color, halfway between the snowy white of their mother and the dark brown of their wild father.

Not all the stories of family pets ended so happily. One Easter the boys bought two adorable Easter chicks, one dyed a bright green, the other bright orange. They took turns feeding and watering them. They cleaned their cage. As the days passed the chicks grew. And grew. And grew! By summertime they'd lost all their colored baby feathers and had become large white roosters parading aggressively around the yard.

One morning, Eddie's mom put his one-year-old brother, Greg, out on the patio to get some sun. He was playing happily when up strutted one of the roosters. His hackles raised and he dropped his head. His spread his wings stiffly to his side and scratched the ground. He looked baby Greg menacingly in the eye. Then, with a rustle and a flash, he leaped into the air and pounced on Greg's head. He dug his sharp claws into Greg's tender scalp and flogged him mercilessly with his stiff wings. Greg let out a cry that you could have heard in the next county!

In two seconds, Little Eddie's dad was out the door and at Greg's side. In another half second, his hand was around that rooster's throat. In one rapid, graceful movement, the rooster rose high overhead and came down with a "Pop". That was the last time he tried to pick a fight with baby Greg.

Little Eddie's Birthdays

The Eastern Box Turtle is one of God's most wonderful creatures. It carries its house around on its back everywhere it goes. But what a house! Box turtle shells are works of art with red, yellow, and orange geometric patterns. Their stubby legs are covered with scales that match the color of their shells. You can tell the males by their bright red or orange eyes; the females have brown eyes.

Little Eddie loved box turtles, so for his sixth birthday he asked to go on a box turtle safari. The family loaded up in their station wagon and, with a basket of sandwiches, headed for the back roads of the county. Appalachia in the springtime is a magical place with fiddleheads of ferns opening and the white surprise of Bloodroot flower bursting through the carpet of last year's leaves. The flowers of the Sarvice tree had come and gone, and now trilliums were lining the folds of the hollows. A spring rain had passed over, and the sun shone wetly through tulip poplar and beech leaves.

As the family rounded a curve they spotted the form of a box turtle making its solemn way across the road. They stopped to pick it up, and it immediately withdrew inside its handsome shell. In a few minutes, the little boys were laughing loudly from the back seat as they watched it poke its head out of its shell and then its feet.

As it got braver, it tried to push away from them, paddling the air with its stumpy feet.

When they got home, Little Eddie's dad got out his hand drill and carefully drilled a small hole through the lip of the turtle's shell, fastening a wire leader to it.

"Does it hurt him?" asked Little Eddie.

"No more than it hurts you to clip your finger nails," said his dad.

They carried the turtle to the grape trellis and tied him to a post with a six-foot length of string. They set him down in the deep grass.

"I'm going to name him Herbie," said Little Eddie. "What does he eat?"

Eddie's dad suggested he try to feed him peanut butter. Eddie ran to the house to fetch a jar and came back panting. He unscrewed the lid and dipped his finger in. He came out with a long whip of peanut butter hanging from his finger. Holding the turtle up, he waved the peanut butter in front of its face.

"Here, Herbie, Herbie, Herbie!" said Little Eddie. "Time for dinner!"

Herbie didn't look especially interested. Eddie waved the peanut butter closer. Still no action. At last, he put the peanut butter right up against Herbie's sharp little beak of a mouth. That was the moment Little Eddie learned an important lesson...Herbie was a meat eater!

The turtle snaked its wrinkly neck out, opened its mouth wide, and bit down on Eddie's finger, clean up to the second joint. Little Eddie let out a shriek and began to swing his arm in a circle. Herbie's little tail straightened out as he orbited Eddie's head, but he held on tight. Some people say a turtle won't let go until it thunders. Little Eddie was getting worried. Fortunately, his dad came to the rescue. He first grabbed Little Eddie, then Herbie, and adopted the same technique he'd used on the rooster. Herbie began to loosen his grip. His red eyes bugged out and finally he let go. Eddie looked down at the bite mark on his finger, then used that finger to wipe his eye.

"Happy Birthday to me." he said with a sniff.

When Little Eddie turned seven, he didn't ask for a box turtle safari. He wanted something different. He wanted to celebrate his birthday in a cave! As it happened, his daddy knew a farmer who owned a pasture with a cave in it.

On May 27th, Little Eddie, his family, and a couple of friends headed out to the country. They parked on a farm lane under a honey locust tree and held the barbed wire up for everyone to crawl under. Carefully dodging brown splats that dotted the pasture, they made their way to an upthrust of lichen covered limestone. Rounding a boulder, they came to a mysterious opening in the side of the hill. A cool breeze flowed from the cave mouth, and on it was a humid, underground sort of smell.

Holding hands, they cautiously entered the cave. Each step took them deeper into the darkness, but as they went, their eyes began to adjust. After a couple of minutes, Little Eddie looked back to see a tiny spot of emerald-green light at the cave mouth. He was mighty glad to be carrying a birthday present he'd opened earlier; a bright red plastic flashlight!

Bit by bit, they advanced over pebbles and rocks. They came to places where stalactites hung from the ceiling and water dripped into glassy pools. They reached a spot where everyone could sit down, and Eddie's mom produced a birthday cake. His dad lit the candles and everyone turned off their flashlights. Eddie made a wish and blew out the candles. Suddenly, it was pitch dark. He couldn't see his hand although it was right in front of his face! He was just starting to feel a little afraid when all of a sudden, one of the candles burst back into flame. Then another, and another. They were trick candles! Little Eddie laughed with relief. He wasn't in any hurry to blow them out again.

On the way out of the cave, Little Eddie spotted something small and furry hanging from the passage wall. He walked closer to look at it, and at that moment it turned to look back at him! It was a Little Brown Bat, one of the species that inhabited their area. At that moment, Eddie turned and said to his dad, "Remember when I blew out my candles? Guess what I wished for.'"

"What?" asked his dad.

"A bat!" said Little Eddie and broke into a grin that lit up the cave.

Little Eddie's dad smiled back at him and produced an empty bread bag. He helped him gently slide it over the Little Brown Bat.

When Little Eddie got home, he took his bat to the spare room. The only piece of furniture was a long table that sat right in the center of the room. Next, he ran to his bedroom and grabbed a sleeping bag. "Come on, boys!" he shouted, "Let's have some fun!" They followed him to the spare room and crawled under the table. Then, before they let the bat loose, they climbed into the sleeping bag. Peeping out from a small hole, they watched Little Eddie undo the twist tie on the bread bag and shake the bat out. It sat bewildered on the floor for about three seconds, then with a series of high-pitched shrieks, it took to the air.

"Where did it go?" asked Scotty.

"Hang on, I'll check," said Eddie. He poked his head out of the sleeping bag. For a second, he saw nothing, then, next thing he knew, the bat was zipping past his face! He ducked back inside the sleeping bag.

"It's out there alright! It's flying in loops under the table!" he said with a shiver. The boys waited for a long time.

"Think it's safe now?" asked Jimmy.

"I'll see," said Little Eddie. He cautiously poked his head out of the sleeping bag. WHOOSH! The bat sailed right past his face. He screamed and jerked his head back inside the bag.

"It's going around in circles!" said Little Eddie. "We're never going to get out of here!"

A few minutes later, the boy's dad heard an unusual racket coming from the spare room. When he went to investigate, he saw a wiggling sleeping bag under the table and a Little Brown Bat flying in loops. He shook his head and smiled. Opening the door wide, he made the bat very happy, but not as happy as he made his three terrified sons!

To Infinity and Beyond!

In front of Little Eddie's house there were five old spruce trees. They looked like Noah might have tied off to them when the flood waters went down. Their trunks were fat and leaked sticky sap that smelled like Christmas. Overhead, their branches stuck out at regular intervals like spokes on a wheel. They were the best climbing trees in the world, so the boys climbed them!

They'd spend summer afternoons perched like crows in the branches, looking down on the roof of their house and across the valley to faraway hillsides. They'd make things from twigs and sap. They'd tell stories. They'd dare each other to climb higher.

One day, Little Eddie got the idea of a contest. He ran into the house and grabbed a red rag. Then, eyeballing the trees to see which was the tallest, he began to shinny skyward. As he ascended, the trunk got thinner and the branches began to get sparse. He stuck the rag in his mouth so he could hold on better with both hands. The house was so far beneath him it looked like a doll's house. The breeze blew and the treetop moved with it.

Squeezing his eyes shut, he inched his way higher. Then, with his last ounce of courage, he hoisted himself to the next branch. Taking the rag from his mouth, he risked his life to remove a hand from the limb in order to tie the rag around it. Amazingly, he didn't fall while tying his flag to the pinnacle of the tree!

He gingerly made his way back down, making sure not to miss any branches. When he got to the bottom, he called his brothers together. Squinting up at the top of the tree, he pointed out the red flag. It looked like something that had been left on the summit of Everest.

"You see that, boys?" he bragged. "I'll bet that's a hundred feet in the air. I dare any of you to climb up there and move it higher!"

Over the months, the red flag was moved higher and higher, inches at a time. Little Eddie and his brothers could have been killed. Why did they do it? Because it was there!

Adventures with Electricity

Little Eddie and his brothers loved science. This got them into a world of trouble over the years. Once Eddie went to a museum where he saw a fascinating piece of equipment called a Jacob's Ladder. It resembled an old Rabbit Ears antenna, with two metal rods projecting out at different angles. A current of electricity was introduced at the bottom and a spark was generated. The spark would arc between the two rods and slowly climb until it snapped out with a pop.

When Eddie got home, he wanted to build his own Jacob's Ladder. He ran to his parent's closet and grabbed a metal clothes hangar. Using an old pair of pliers from his dad's toolbox, he managed to untwist the wire and then bend it in the shape of a triangle. It wasn't exactly a Jacob's Ladder, but to Little Eddie, it looked close enough.

Just as he was about to insert both ends of the coat hanger into a wall outlet, his dad happened to walk by. Good thing he did! At best, Little Eddie would have blown all the fuses and spent the rest of the evening sitting in the dark. At the worst, he'd have spent the rest of eternity sitting somewhere else!

Little Eddie's mom had a big old clothes dryer that sat in the corner of the kitchen. It ran on 220 watts of electricity, enough to kill a full-grown man, not to mention Little Eddie. It was a bit cantankerous and would remind you who was boss by giving you a shock when you least expected it.

Little Eddie's mom also liked to make homemade whole-wheat bread from time to time. She'd mix the ingredients in a stainless steel pot, then sift out some flour on the old brown kitchen table and go to kneading. She had this way of furrowing her brow and biting her lower lip when she kneaded that dough. It always gave Little Eddie the suspicious feeling she was taking out some of her motherly frustration. Fortunately, it was on the bread instead of him.

After she finished kneading, she would hoist the old pot to the top of the refrigerator where it stayed just the right temperature for the dough to rise. The only thing was, with five little boys running around the place, intent on killing themselves or someone else, she'd often lose track of the time and forget her rising dough.

It was just Little Eddie's bad luck that someone had shown him pictures at school from a horror movie called "The Blob." This hideous creature from outer space would creep up on unsuspecting victims and suck the life out of them. So what was he to think when he jogged into the kitchen to get a drink and looked up towards the refrigerator? There it was! The Blob! It was crawling over the sides of the pot, sliding down the side of the fridge, and reaching for him!

Without thinking, Little Eddie took a step backward...right into the clutches of the electric clothes dryer. There was a blue flash and a smell of ozone. Little Eddie stiffened out like a board. Fortunately, as he toppled over, he fell away from the dryer instead of into it. If he had, this would be the last story in this book.

Little Eddie's parents had reached another anniversary in their marriage and felt they deserved to celebrate. They planned to go off on a hiking trip, alone, for a couple of days, so they hired a teenage girl from the neighborhood to watch the boys.

Eddie didn't feel like he could trust his family's safety to one teenage girl. Why, any number of things could happen. Dastardly villains, thieves, robbers, and crooks could be lurking about in the dark right outside the window! He and the boys came up with a plan. They found two extension cords and cut an end off each one. Then, they carefully twisted the exposed wires from the two ends together. Finally, they plugged the end of one cord into an outlet and spread the prongs of the other end so that it'd fit snugly around the metal handle of their aluminum storm door. That ought to take care of any bad guys who wanted to sneak in during the night. One touch on that handle, and a robber would light up like a Christmas tree!

It didn't quite work out like that though. The prongs of the plug had not made a good contact on the aluminum door handle at first. It wasn't until the babysitter walked into the room to see what the boys were up to that the excitement began. As she approached the door, her foot hit the cord. Immediately blue and white sparks shot across the room as thick clouds of white smoke billowed upward and fanned across the ceiling. An acrid smell filled the room. Although you couldn't see your hand in front of your face for the smoke, someone had the presence of mind to follow the extension cord back to the outlet and give it a hard pull.

The zapping noise quieted down, and the last spark fell to the floor. The boys opened some windows and doors to help clear the smoke out. When at last they could make out some shapes, they saw the figure of the baby sitter staring intently at the storm door. The handle had melted almost completely in two and was hanging at a sad angle toward the floor. She didn't speak for the longest time, and when she did, it wasn't to thank the boys for trying to protect her from the bad guys. She just shook her head and mumbled, "How am I going to explain this to your parents?"

Swiss Family Robinson

Little Eddie's life wasn't just wild adventures and harrowing escapes. He enjoyed the times when his mom would read to him and his brothers in front of the fireplace. It was better than watching Batman on T.V!

Eddie and his brothers would stretch out on the rug in front of a warm fire. Chin in hand, they gazed into the embers and jumped when a log popped, throwing sparks up the chimney. Their mom would settle into an old armchair and pick up a copy of Swiss Family Robinson from the end table beside her. Then they'd start into chapter seventeen, or twenty-three, or thirty-six. The stories were amazing! Shipwrecks, tree houses, giant snakes, crystal caverns. In the active imaginations of Little Eddie and his brothers, the stories were better than Hollywood, and they pictured themselves as the stars.

As Little Eddie grew older, it was Narnia and Aslan called to his heart, and he kept his eyes open for portals and magic doors that lead to magical worlds. Maybe it was a good way to calm down a bunch of wiggling boys, but little did their mother know, it was giving her sons great ideas for their next adventures.

Chapter Two
Seth, West Virginia, 1967-69, Age 11-13

The Palace at Rock Castle Holler

When President Lyndon Johnson declared war on poverty in the 1960's, Little Eddie's dad was one of the first to enlist. He packed the family up and moved from the coalfields of southwestern Virginia to the coal fields of southern West Virginia. They settled on the banks of the Big Coal River in Boone County, one of the poorest places in all of Appalachia. The silty river threaded its way between steep eroded hills where folks only saw the sun for a few hours each day. Following the river closely through its twists and turns was a train track for hauling out coal. Between the river and the railroad ran a pot-holed highway that linked one small mining community to the next.

Seth was one such town. The poor section was a mining camp called Rock Castle Holler. Over the millennia, the small stream that flowed through the holler had eaten its way down through layers of sandstone and coal to leave impressive cliffs and bulwarks that reminded someone of a castle. Small miners houses, that looked like anything but a castle, were huddled along the banks of the creek. In one of them Little Eddie was to eat his first and only pickled-pig's-ear-on-white-bread-with-yellow-mustard sandwich.

Fortunately for Little Eddie, his father found a nicer place to rent. It was the supervisor's house, situated out of the holler on a shoulder of the hill with views to the Upper and Lower Turnhole of the river. The word "nicer" must be taken in context, because the house didn't have indoor plumbing. Instead, it had a little one-seater outhouse in a corner of the back yard. The house was graced with a large front porch that looked out on two old maple trees. It was sided with thousands of weathered pine shingles. Walking in the front door, you couldn't help but notice the hallway leading to the back bedrooms rolled up and down and plaster had fallen in places from the ceiling. It had a faint air of faded glory evidenced by peeling white pillars in the living room and diamond paned windows that were mostly intact. Not bad, really for fifteen dollars a month in rent!

Sammy Dunlap and the Water Dog

In time, Little Eddie got to know the neighbors. Ten-year-old Clifford Green, for instance, lived two doors down in a house that wasn't nearly so nice. At school, everyone called Clifford "Devil" Green. He had an evil eye he squinched and could not focus. His dark hair looked like it had been cut by his little sister with garden shears. His face was usually dirty. Clifford's nickname came not so much from his looks but from his temperament. He was a formidable rock thrower, and the battles he fought with Little Eddie and the boys were epic. To add insult to injury, Clifford nearly busted a gut laughing the time his diaper-less baby brother peed off their front porch, giving Eddie a shower.

The house next door to Little Eddie's was a weathered two-story building that always seemed to be leaning slightly. Granny Dunlap lived there with her grandson, Sammy. He acted like a forty-year-old man in a sixteen-year-old body. Eddie had never paid attention to an Adam's apple until he met Sammy. Above it sat two dark eyes that peered from behind horn-rimmed glasses. Sammy shaved...sometimes.

On weekends Little Eddie would hear gunshots coming from next door. It wasn't that unusual in Rock Castle Holler, but one day he asked Sammy what was going on. Sammy explained that he loved staying up late to watch "Triple Chiller" on T.V, a weekend feature of B grade horror reruns. He would stretch out on his saggy couch with a bottle of RC Cola and his .22 rifle propped up between his toes. Every now and then, he'd turn his head to check a mouse hole in the corner. If a mouse popped its head out, he would "pop" it. That explained a lot.

Sammy was a gold mine of information. He taught Little Eddie how to butcher a chicken. First he let Little Eddie catch one, which was the hardest part. Then, he would choose a sharp knife from the kitchen drawer and march out to the clothesline in the backyard. With a piece of string, he tied the chicken's feet together and suspended it, head down, from the line. He grabbed the chicken by the head and stretched its neck down. With a flash the knife came down, and Sammy jumped back. The bird exploded in a storm of flapping wings. It kept flapping for a minute until it hung still at last. Sammy explained that if you didn't hang it from the clothesline, it would run around without its head.

Sammy also taught Little Eddie how to make his own lead sinkers. Sinkers are the weights you put on your fishing line to make the bait go down. The way Sammy fished, he needed heavy duty ones and they had to be just right. While Sammy's grandma was away, he and Eddie sneaked into the kitchen and found an old pan. That was the easy part of the job because ALL Granny's pans were old. Sammy put the pan on the stove and lit a gas burner. Then he pulled out a piece of lead pipe from his pocket and dropped it in the pan. For a long time, nothing seemed to happen. Then, it moved and a shiny molten pool began to spread across the bottom of the pan. As the rest of the lead was melting, Sammy began to make little loops out of twist ties that you find on bread bags. When all was ready, he carried the pan to the back yard and carefully dibbled out some holes in the dirt with a stick. As he poured molten lead into the holes, Little

Eddie was supposed to insert the wire loop into each one before it cooled. It was tricky work because if he hurried he could get burned and if he waited the lead would cool and the wire wouldn't go in. After a few minutes, Sammy gingerly grabbed one of the wire loops and pulled up. A beautiful new sinker popped out of the dirt, glinting in the sun like a silver nugget. Those sinkers were beautiful, but later on in life, Little Eddie learned that breathing the fumes from molten lead could cause brain damage. That explained a few things about Sammy.

"Now," said Sammy, "It's time I taught you how to go cat fishin'."

Little Eddie couldn't wait to go cat fishin'!

That Friday night, Sammy stopped by to get Little Eddie. He was carrying three cheap Zebco 202 rod and reels, a bucket of fishing supplies, and a brown paper bag. Eddie had gotten permission to go fishing with Sammy, though he'd be up past his normal bedtime. Perhaps it was because they didn't have to go far, just two hundred feet down the hill to the Lower Turnhole. If they got in trouble, they could always holler for help. They walked down the path through the strawberry patch and crossed the railroad tracks. Then they slid down a steep bank and landed on a little bluff above the river. At this point, the river was about fifty feet wide and it took a hard turn to the right. This carved out a deep hole of swirling water, thus the name "Turnhole." In the fading light, Sammy found an old tire, stuffed it with some newspaper, and lit it on fire. This was long before most people were aware of the environment. Instead of being concerned about the thick cloud of black smoke rising into the night, Eddie delighted in the hellish blaze and steady hiss and pop of the burning tire. It cast an eerie glow across the moving water and provided light for Sammy to cut some forked sticks to prop up the poles. From the paper bag Sammy removed two RC Colas and a white plastic container.

"Right there's our secret weapon," he said. "There ain't a catfish alive that can resist chicken livers."

Little Eddie peered into the tub as Sammy pried off the lid. The raw chicken livers looked bloody and disgusting. His stomach gave a squeamish flip, but he tried to be brave. He wondered what a catfish saw in chicken livers.

In a few minutes, the lines were cast out and the rods set up in their sticks. Sammy had reeled them in just enough to tighten the lines and bend the rod tip slightly. The least little nibble would be telegraphed to the tip of the rod, whereupon Sammy instructed Eddie to, "Jerk his eyeteeth out!"

The minutes slipped by, but Eddie kept his laser like focus on the gleaming rod tip. Without letting his eyes leave the rod, he took a swig of RC Cola. Then he took another. Then he had to take a pee in the bushes.

All of a sudden he heard Sammy shout and the sound of a fishing rod whipping the air. Little Eddie raced back to see him struggling with his reel, his line slicing the oily-looking surface of the dark water. After a minute, something broke the surface. Eddie expected to see the broad back and whiskered face of a catfish, but he was in for a shock. Instead, what came writhing up on the muddy bank was something he'd never seen before. It looked like some prehistoric leviathan; wrinkled and brown with stubby legs protruding from the side and hideous external gills rising from behind its jaws. It's tiny eyes glowed red in the firelight lending it a diabolical air. It opened its toothless mouth wide in an effort to throw the hook and writhed from side to side. Little Eddie was terrified.

"Water Dog!" yelled Sammy. "Get the knife!"

Little Eddie scrambled up the bank to the tackle box, grabbed Sammy's old pocket knife, and returned panting. His eyes opened wide as Sammy lifted the knife, but it was only to cut the line. He wasn't going to put his hand near the water dog! With a loud splash, the enormous amphibian dropped back into the water and sluggishly disappeared into the mysterious depths.

Sammy and Little Eddie flopped down on the wet bank, exhausted.

"I thought you were going to teach me about cat fishin'," said Little Eddie.

"What do you think were doin'?" asked Sammy.

"That wasn't no catfish. That was a dog. A water dog!"

Cussing the Trees

Little Eddie's mom would not have approved of him saying, "That wasn't no catfish." She had studied English in college and insisted her boys speak properly in the house. She understood the other kids might make fun of her boys if they didn't say "ain't" or "wasn't no." So she let them use the local dialect when they were out and about. Inside the house, it was the Queen's English.

One day Little Eddie came home with a new word. "Momma," he asked, "What does this word mean?

"What word?"

"Sh-t"

To her credit, Eddie's mom didn't bat an eye. She sat him down and explained that it was a bathroom word, but it was considered a bad word; a "cuss" word. She didn't allow cuss words in her house either.

Over time, Little Eddie learned a number of cuss words. He heard them everywhere. His friends at school and up the holler were not only fluent, they were artists. They could cuss a blue streak. They were Shakespeares of dirty language, and it made Eddie just a bit jealous that they could cuss and he couldn't. He brought this injustice up with his mom.

"Oh," she said pleasantly, "You are allowed to cuss. All you want. But under one condition."

"What's that?"

"You must go a long way out into the woods where no one can hear you."

A smile crept across little Little Eddie's face and he moved toward the door. He ran outside and up the hill, flushed with excitement. He held his tongue until he'd hiked a quarter mile into the woods and was in no danger of anyone hearing him. It took a moment to get his breath back, but when he did, he turned and faced a big poplar tree. Raring back he gave it everything he had. He cussed it up one side and down the other. He half expected the bark to start flying. It felt good!

Then he turned and tackled an oak tree. Then a maple. He cussed until he he was out of breath, waited a minute, and then started back up again. He cussed a dogwood and a hickory. Finally, when he could cuss no more he stood still and let the quietness of the woods wash around him. He'd cussed himself completely out and felt strangely clean and empty. He was relieved and at peace.

After that, when he had the urge, he'd go back out to the woods for another session. The trees never seemed to mind.

Fight!

Little Eddie's brother, Scotty, was brilliant. He'd skipped a grade in school and still made straight A's. He wore dark, horn rim glasses and tended to be just a bit overweight. He talked about things no one else in school understood. He was a target for bullies.

Ernie lived around the hillside from where Eddie and Scotty lived. He was a couple of grades ahead of Scott. He stood head and shoulders above him. He had muscles and an Adam's apple. He chewed tobacco. Ernie was a bully, and he decided he didn't like Scotty.

One day, Ernie informed Scotty he was going to beat him up. He was generous about it though; he'd let Scotty pick the time and place. Little Eddie was afraid Ernie was going to kill his brother. Why, Ernie might just decide to kill Eddie while he was at it! Eddie knew that big brothers were supposed to stick up for their little brothers, but he had to admit he was afraid. What should he do? What should Scotty do?

"I'm going to fight him," said Scotty, matter of factly.

"He could kill you!" said Eddie.

"What are you going to do?" asked Scotty.

Eddie looked embarrassed and pushed the dirt around with his shoe. An idea came to him.

"I'll referee." If things got out of hand, at least he could run get a gown-up.

The day of the fight came. Ernie strolled through the front gate of the house with a cruel gleam in his eye. He'd been looking forward to this for some time. In a patch of shade, Little Eddie had marked off the ring in the or-chard grass. He explained that he would referee the fight. It was to be a clean fight with no kicking or gouging. Ernie waited impatiently to begin. Scotty, in one of the bravest acts Eddie had ever seen, removed his glasses and stepped into the ring.

As Ernie spat out his tobacco and raised his fists, Scotty charged him unexpectedly, and Ernie went over. In a half second, Scotty wrapped his stocky legs around Ernie's chest and locked his ankles together. Then he began to squeeze. Ernie thumped Scotty with his fists, but Scotty held on. He thrashed from side to side, but Scotty held on. He dragged Scotty through the dirt, but Scotty held on. After a couple of minutes, Ernie's face started to turn red and his eyes bugged out. His Adam's apple bobbed up and down as he struggled to breathe. His flailing got weaker and his eyes widened. Ernie looked over at Eddie and signaled for a time out.

"There aren't any time outs," said Eddie, making up the rules as he went.

"O.K, the fight's over then."

Little Eddie tapped Scotty on the shoulder and he re-leased his strangle hold. Both boys slowly got to their feet. Ernie dusted himself off and looked over at Scotty with a new respect. Then, without saying anything else, he headed out the gate and home.

"Who won?" asked Scotty. Eddie looked at him with pure admiration.

"I don't know," he said, "but you sure didn't lose." As Scotty replaced his glasses, Eddie threw his arm around Scotty's shoulder and proudly walked him back inside the house.

The Ice Titanic

You've heard the story of the Titanic that hit the iceberg, but have you heard the story of the Titanic that WAS an iceberg?

It was one of the coldest winters anyone could remember, so cold that the flowing water of the Big Coal River began to thicken and freeze. Bits of ice clumped together like snowballs. The snowballs lumped together into mats. The mats joined to form ice rafts that bobbed through the rapids. In time, they reached the great bend of the Turnhole where their inertia carried them to the bank. There, they began to stack up and freeze solid. Bit by bit, the icy fringe grew from a few feet to twenty. The ice got thicker and harder. When Little Eddie and the boys discovered it one Saturday morning, it called to them for adventure.

Little Eddie knew how dangerous it was to walk out onto ice, not because you could slip and fall, but because it could break and send you tumbling into icy water. If you fell through this river ice, the current would carry you along underneath the ice and you couldn't come up for air!

Eddie's little brothers didn't know about the dangers of ice, so he carefully explained it to them. Instead of walking out on the ice, they would have to content themselves with throwing rocks onto it. They began with small rocks that bounced and skittered until they disappeared into the running water at the edge of the ice. Then, they looked for bigger rocks to throw. Those rocks also bounced and slid across the ice. Finally, determined to put a hole in the ice, they found the biggest rock they could lift and gave it a heave from the top of the bank. It thundered down and hit the ice with a thud. Nothing. Not even a tiny crack.

Little Eddie figured that if the ice could support a rock that weighed three times what any of them weighed, it could support them. He carefully stepped onto the white surface. Nothing. He took a little jump. Nothing. He took a big jump. Solid as a rock.

So, for the next twenty minutes, Eddie and the boys whooped and hollered and skated back and forth across their personal ice rink. When they tired of that, Eddie got an idea. He ran up the bank, across the railroad tracks, through the snowy strawberry patch to the house to fetch his dad's camp hatchet. When he got back, he set to work chopping through the thick ice.

"What are you doing?" his brothers asked as he extended the length of his cut.

"You'll see," he said, and kept chopping.

Bit by bit he cut through the ice until at last he had freed up a large chunk in the shape of a boat. Running back up the bank, he quickly cut several poles and returned.

"Jump on for a ride on the Titanic!" He yelled. Using the poles, they pushed themselves out into the current, and before they knew it, they were a hundred yards downstream. The icy water bubbled and slid past them. They used the poles to fend off from the bank and away from submerged rocks. They were having a grand time!

A quarter mile down the river, they heard an ominous cracking sound. Looking down at their feet they saw a nearly invisible split grow and grow until dark water appeared between the two pieces. They had to act quickly! Judging one piece to be larger than the other, they jumped across the widening crack. Saved!

But not for long. What the boys didn't know was that running water has a lower freezing point than still water. The shallow rapids they were approaching would melt their ship! Crack! The ice broke in half again, and again the boys leaped for the larger piece. It wasn't very big, and as they moved from side to side, part would disappear underwater as the opposite side rose in the air. The rock they hit only hurried the inevitable, and the boys jumped for the bank. The icy water took their breath away, and they were mighty glad it was only waist deep. Helping one another through the rocks and eddies, they finally splashed ashore. Fortunately, they fetched up on the correct side of the river. Unfortunately, they had to jog nearly a half-mile through the bitter cold in freezing wet clothes. Fortunately, everyone made it home, some bluer than others.

When their mother learned what had happened, she couldn't make up her mind. She knew the boys needed warming up, she just couldn't decide whether to do it with a spanking spoon or with hugs of gratitude to God. Fortunately, grace won the day; grace that they avoided drowning and grace that they weren't given the whipping they deserved!

The Fur-lined Toilet Seat

The outhouse was an important feature in American history for hundreds of years. It was a humble place, with its share of earthy odors. But it was also a place for refuge and reflection, a place where you could receive revelation and new insights. It turned out to be just that for Miss Dorothy, but we're getting ahead of ourselves...

An outhouse can be a pleasant place to pass the time on a warm afternoon in late spring. But on a bitter cold winter evening, well, let's just say it's a different story. It's not quite so bad if you don't have to sit down...which the boys did only occasionally. But for Little Eddie's mother, the winter trips to the outhouse were another matter. And, being the daughter of an inventor, she wasn't going to take the matter sitting down!

On one of her trips to town, she stopped at a rummage sale. While there, she saw an old coat with a huge raccoon collar. Her mental wheels started spinning and her eyes lit up. She gave the clerk ten cents for the coat, rushed home, removed the collar, cut out a horseshoe shaped piece of cardboard, and glued the fur to it. Voila! A fur-lined toilet seat. She marched out to the outhouse with a hammer and nail, and before long that outhouse was accessorized with the most glamorous seat in the county...maybe the state, hanging there on its nail.

Little Eddie and his brothers admired their mother's ingenuity and quickly recognized that sometimes they had to sit down too. They asked their mother if she would share her fur-lined toilet seat.

"Not on your life!" she said. "I know you boys and what you'll do. You'll forget to hang it back on its nail, and then the next one will come along and pee all over it. Go find your own fur-lined-toilet seat."

Well, those fur-lined-toilet seats didn't just grow on trees, and after a couple of weeks of cold backsides and constant complaining, she finally caved in.

"Just remember...always hang it back on it's nail!"

Miss Dorothy moved with her husband and two children from New Jersey to the next town down the river. She was a large woman of Italian descent. The boys admired her faint mustache and the expressive way she talked. She loved talking, with her hands or any other way, but found that the local women were stand-offish. Little Eddie's mother, on the other hand, never met a stranger.

So Miss Dorothy would drive up once or twice a week to sit in the kitchen, drink a cup of coffee, and chat with her friend. She never stayed for too long, and the boys wondered if it had anything to do with her fear of the outhouse. After all, outhouses could be dangerous places, what with Black Widow spider bites and methane gas explosions. But one afternoon, the conversation was just too interesting, and one hour stretched into two. One cup of coffee stretched into another. At last, Miss Dorothy had to answer nature's call, and she was certain she'd never make it home without an accident. Mustering all her courage, she asked, "O.K. Where is your bathroom?"

"Oh, we don't have a bathroom," the boys replied innocently. "We have an outhouse."

"I know that," snapped Miss Dorothy impatiently. The urgency was building. "Where is your "outhouse"?"

The boys spilled onto the rickety back porch, reached up to pull the string on the naked bulb that swung from overhead, and peered out through the gathering dusk.

"You see that little building over there in the corner of the yard?" they asked.

"Barely," answered Miss Dorothy.

"Well, that's it." Little Eddie and the boys left her to it and went back in the kitchen.

Moments later, they were shocked to hear an ear-piercing scream. It was right up there in decibels alongside a Navy fighter jet, and it had an eerie, supernatural quality to it. The boys nearly broke the door down in their rush to the back porch. In the gloom, they could just make out the bulky shape of Miss Dorothy. She was defying gravity in jumps nearly six feet off the ground, which was amazing because her underwear was still wrapped around her ankles.

"AAAAAHHH!" she shrieked. "AAAaatacked. Something attacked me in there!

When at long last, Little Eddie picked himself up off the ground and managed to control his laughter, he turned to his brothers and asked the question, "O.K...Who forgot to hang up the fur-lined toilet seat?"

Burning Down the House

The summer dragged on. It seemed even longer because Little Eddie's mom would not allow him and his brothers to spend all day in front of the T.V. She said it would turn their minds to Jello. So, they looked for other ways to keep busy.

The boys usually looked to Little Eddie, and he didn't want to let them down. He had a plan.

"Hey, guys. We could go out back and dig some deep trenches. Then we could lay boards across the top and put the dirt back on. If each one works on his section, we could connect them and make an underground network of tunnels. We could widen some to be sleeping chambers with holes for candles in the walls. We could disappear for weeks!"

Off they ran to the tool shed, and in no time, shovelfuls of dirt were flying through the air. They dug steadily through the heat of the afternoon, and by nightfall they'd opened up the hillside four or five feet. The blisters on their hands gave them a satisfied feeling of accomplishment. They were sure that by the next evening they'd be sleeping underground.

The next morning they hit bedrock. It was one of those moments of crushing disappointment that come to everyone. It just hits harder when you're only in elementary school. Little Eddie looked around at his crestfallen siblings and felt their frustration. He suspected they were beginning to doubt his leadership. He had to come up with Plan B...fast!

At that moment, his eyes fell on the impressive heap of dirt that had been piled up. In a moment of inspiration, ready to make lemonade from lemons, he leapt on top of the pile.

"Boys, we might not get our tunnels, but look at what we've accomplished. We've stacked up this mighty mountain of dirt. With a little work, we could carve out a crater in the top, make a miniature forest of twigs, and put a model native village at the bottom. We'd have our own volcano!"

The boys weren't completely convinced, but as they turned their attention to the volcano, they warmed to the project. The crater was convincing. So was the miniature forest and the native village. They stepped back to admire their work. Something was missing...what could it be? When Little Eddie suggested red hot lava, the boys erupted with cheers.

They raced to the tool shed, found an old bucket, and began looking for anything that might burn. Of special interest were the containers marked, "Caution. Extremely flammable. Keep away from fire!" They were thrilled to find a bottle of purple art goop their mother used to create artificial flowers. It would add just the desired effect, but they wanted more. It was then Scotty recalled the chemistry set he'd received for Christmas. It was up in the attic! Without hesitating, the boys dashed inside, through the kitchen, and up the narrow back stairs to the attic. They examined each small vial of chemicals, choosing only the ones that would burn and poured their contents into a test tube. For want of a Bunsen burner, they lit a candle, placed it in a Dixie cup, and began to heat the test tube. When it was bubbling properly, they dumped its contents into the bucket and ran down the stairs and out the door. They poured the mixture into the crater and stepped back. Eddie struck a match and tossed it in.

KA-FWOOOM! The earth shook as a blast of flame rose six feet into the air. The miniature village trembled. Smoke rolled. And in a final burst of glory, the purple art goop began to boil and roll over the lip of the crater, setting the tiny forest on fire. It was sensational and the boys reveled in their triumph.

Volcanic eruptions are hot work, especially on an August afternoon, and Little Eddie and the boys had worked up a thirst. They headed inside to find their mom chatting over a cup of coffee with the minister. Each one grabbed a chipped cup or an old Mason jar and filled it from the sink. They dropped into chairs around the kitchen table and tried not to interrupt.

But it didn't last long. Baby Gray got restless and toddled out onto the back porch. In a minute he toddled back in. He pulled on his momma's sleeve and looked anxiously up into her face.

"Momma," he said. "Moke...moke inna window."

"Honey," said his mother, "Don't interrupt me when I'm talking to the preacher."

Gray was an obedient little boy. He didn't interrupt any more, but he wandered back out to the porch. When the preacher had finished his coffee and said his good-byes, the boy's mother stepped out on the back porch to collect laundry from the wringer washer. In less than a second, the door banged open and she yelled.

"Smoke! There's smoke coming out of the attic window!"

Little Eddie and the boys stampeded out the back door and looked up at the attic window. Sure enough, there WAS a thick cloud of dark smoke pouring through the upstairs window. Immediately, Little Eddie grabbed the bucket that was lying beside the volcano and headed back into the kitchen. It seemed to take forever to fill at the sink, but finally he dashed to the door to the attic steps and jerked it open. A blast of heat struck him in the face, and he stared into a roiling holocaust of flame. With a heave, he flung the bucket of water up the stairway, but it only sizzled. A tongue of fire began to spread across the yellowed wallpaper of the kitchen ceiling.

Forget the attic! It was now every man for himself. Little Eddie ran to the boys' bedroom. They all shared a dresser and Eddie's clothes were in the top drawer. He didn't have time to run down the hall. Every second was precious. So he grabbed a chair and did something he'd always wanted to do. He threw it threw the window! His drawer full of clothes followed close behind. But just as he was reaching for Scotty's drawer, he remembered his new fishing pole. He couldn't let it burn up!

Meanwhile, Scotty had run to the living room and was selflessly rescuing the set of Encyclopedia Britannica, one armload at a time. Neighbors began to gather. A young Marine, home on furlough, and another gentleman hauled the Steinway upright piano through the front doors, manhandled it down the stairs, and left it propped against one of the large maple trees by the gate. Little Eddie thought his superhero dad might have done it by himself, if he'd been there, but he was away in Charleston at a meeting for the day.

Burning chunks of ceiling began to drop into the hallway and the tarpaper on the roof had become a black Niagara Falls. The boy's mom refused to let them go back inside. A fire truck had been called from Whitesville, fifteen miles away, and by the time it arrived, the back half of the house was ablaze. Firemen leapt out and cranked up the pump on their tanker truck. They began to direct a steady stream of water onto the roof. More neighbors arrived. Little Eddie added to the festive occasion by sitting down at the piano and playing ragtime music. Everything appeared to be under control.

Until the tanker truck went dry! The firemen glanced about, but they weren't surprised not to find a hydrant in Rock Castle Holler. No problem. They were prepared. In a moment, two burly firemen were lugging a portable pump down the hill, through the strawberry patch, across the railroad tracks, to the riverbank. They connected a hose, and in minutes a fresh stream of water was being directed to the roof, or what was left of it. Eddie started to play again.

Just then, a far-off sound reached their ears. It was strangely familiar. Following the direction of the sound, their eyes went down the hill, through the strawberry patch, to the railroad tracks. THAT'S what makes a noise like that! A train whistle!

Sure enough, the 5:15 train, loaded with over one hundred cars of coal, was barreling down the stretch. Then everyone's eyes followed the fire hose as it went down the hill, through the strawberry patch, and across the railroad tracks.

Well, there's no way to stop a fully loaded coal train traveling at 50 miles an hour in less than a mile and a half, certainly not before it ran over the fire hose, slicing it cleanly in two. On one side of the tracks, the cut hose thrashed about, spraying water in all directions. On the other side, the fireman directing the nozzle watched his stream of water die away to nothing. Any hopes to save the house died with it.

By the time the hose was spliced, the house was gone. Six steps climbed bravely to where the front porch had been and gave way to a smoking ash heap. The chimney stood sadly off to one side. A kind neighbor lady put her arm around the boy's mother and invited them to walk down the hill to her house for some supper.

No one was home when Little Eddie's father arrived. He pulled up to the empty lot where his home had been. There was a piano under the maple tree, but that was about it. Getting out of the car he followed the walkway to the front steps. He circled the ash heap, passing the chimney. He made his way to the back yard and saw something that puzzled him. There, not twenty feet from the smoldering remains of his home, was a small volcano, purple lava still cooling on its sides. He looked back at the ashes of his home, then turned to stare again at the volcano. He scratched his head in wonder.

"Could it be?" he asked himself. "Could it really be?"

Chapter Three
Racine, West Virginia,
1969-74, Age 13-18

The House on Racine Hill

After the house in Rock Castle Holler burned to the ground, Eddie's family needed a new place to live. For a few weeks they had to divide up, staying with friends, sleeping on couches and the floor. That was how Eddie came to eat a pickled-pig's—ear-on-white-bread-with-yellow-mustard sandwich. Eddie's brothers were mad at him because he'd managed to save his clothes from the fire but not theirs. They were all wearing odds and ends from the Goodwill store.

One day, Eddie's dad came back from house hunting with news. He'd found a place! It was three miles down the river from where they'd been living. It was a "house" on twenty-seven acres of land selling for only $4,000. The reason it was so cheap was because the house had officially been condemned.

They piled into the station wagon and headed to Racine. Turning off the highway at a gas station, they crossed the river on a steel bridge. Next they bumped across the railroad tracks and climbed through the small community of Racine. Taking a sharp left above the town, they threaded their way along a narrow dirt road. On their right, shale cliffs hugged the road, to the left was a hundred foot drop to the railroad tracks. After a mile, the road descended to a small hollow and crossed a creek. Above them on a promontory they could make out an old farmhouse.

They parked the car on the road because the long driveway up the hill was impassable. After a walk up the rutted drive they came out on the crown of the hill. It was grown up with golden ragweed. Here and there pink flowers of Joe Pye weed waved on long stalks, interspersed with the deep indigo of Ironweed flowers. A huge white oak shaded the front yard and an ancient apple tree stood by the double front porch. Another sheltered the back corner.

The house was two stories with peeling board and batten siding. It was square in shape with a simple floor plan. Two good-sized rooms downstairs, two upstairs, and a couple of rooms tacked on to the back as an afterthought. None of the rooms was a bathroom. The house had no framework; it's style of construction was called "Jenny Lynn". There were the outside boards and inside boards; no insulation between, and in the winters the head of each nail that penetrated the wall would be beaded with ice. The house was "heated" by radiant gas heaters, one in each room. They were wonderful to cozy up to after coming in from the outside.

As the boys' dad carefully opened the back door and poked his head inside, his eyes began to shine. He knocked the cobwebs aside and walked through the kitchen. He climbed the narrow stairs to the upper floor. He opened the door to the upstairs porch, but declined to risk his neck stepping out. He descended to the dining room and then finished his tour in the living room. Turning with a smile, he looked at his family. Just as he was about to make a pronouncement, he fell through the floor! Right down to the ground. Fortunately, he wasn't hurt. His head was still sticking above the floor, and he looked up at his wife and children. With the voice of a love-struck teenager he said, "We'll take it!"

The Dumb Class

School had started by this time, and their parents took the boys to enroll them in their new classes. Each one was assigned a teacher and a classroom until it came time for Eddie. The eighth grade, it seemed, was big enough for two classes, and it had been divided according to the students' academic ability; the smart class and the dumb class. Eddie might not have been that smart, but he was smart enough to worry when they said there was only space left in the dumb class.

As it turned out, Eddie learned a good deal in the dumb class. He picked up more interesting vocabulary. He learned about shaving from his classmate, Roger. He picked up some anatomy lessons every time the teacher left the room because another boy would drop his pants and run around the room.

Most of the kids in Eddie's class were bored with school. They were looking for something to do, and what they liked best was to beat up Eddie! Eddie, for some odd reason, wasn't so fond of this activity.

Dances With Ponies

All the attention at his new school made Eddie lonesome for his old school, and his old friends. One friend in particular was a cute, brown haired girl named Debbie Donohue. She had a big-eyed little sister named Bama that was a good friend of Jimmy's.

So when the boy's acquired a couple of ponies for their new farm, it wasn't that surprising that Eddie and Jimmy asked to ride them to visit their girlfriends.

"So, where do these girls live?" asked their mom.

"Up Prenter Holler," answered Eddie.

"Isn't that about seven miles from here?" she asked with a dubious look on her face.

"Yes, but it'll be a little shorter if we take the train tracks."

To this day, Eddie wonders what convinced his mother to let them go, but she did. They had no saddles for the ponies, and their backs were as bony as a skeleton. As they rode along the side of the tracks, Eddie motivated Jimmy by reminding him how cute little Bama was, and Jimmy did the same for Eddie.

After a couple of hours, the boys stiffly dismounted in the Donohue yard to the amazement of Debbie and Bama. They weren't nearly as excited to see the boys as Eddie hoped they'd be. Perhaps it was because they smelled so strongly of sweat; both boy and pony! Perhaps it was because they could hardly move. Anyway, they had to turn around and head home before the sun got too low.

The ride back was murder, and not just on the ponies. There were no pictures of Debbie and Bama dancing in the boy's heads to urge them on. There were only the blisters growing where the saddles should have been. A "seven-mile" trip up the holler was turning into a fourteen mile nightmare. Just as the last bit of daylight faded from the sky, Eddie and Jimmy dragged themselves up the hill. They limped into the house and collapsed around the kitchen table.

"Well, how was it?" their mother asked.

"Let's put it like this," said Eddie. "We're through with women for a while!"

Those ponies never forgave the boys for that fourteen-mile ride. They never considered themselves beasts of burden, but there was one thing they could bear... a grudge! They were the orneriest ponies for miles around, and they had a mind of their own. When you wanted them to go left, they turned right. When you had in mind a nice trot up the holler, they would turn tail and head home, often throwing the boys head-first over their tails.

One time, Eddie was out for a ride with his brother, Scotty. They'd followed the road a mile around the hillside to the next small town called Bloomingrose. There, they turned around and headed for home. Something about the idea of home always seemed to inspire those ponies.

The road around the hillside was mostly dirt and gravel. However, there were spots where the county had paved it. Those were the places where it dropped steeply into a holler, jumped a culvert, and pulled a couple of G's through a tight curve and up the opposite hill. As Eddie and Scotty approached home, they had to dip through one last holler, and it was there that Eddie's pony got the "goin' home" itch. It started to pick up its speed and broke into a trot along the gravel straightaway.

As he hit the pavement at the top of the hill, Eddie pulled back on the reigns. Without a saddle, it was a little tricky to stay on a pony, especially one that was trotting downhill. His pony ignored him. In fact, it picked up speed, breaking into a gallop. As the pony's nose tilted down the hill, Eddie's nose followed. The pony stretched its neck out and flattened its ears to its head. With each stride, Eddie felt himself sliding inch by inch up over the pony's withers.

"Whoa! Whoa ya dang mule!" shouted Eddie. He could just as well have been speaking Mandarin.

Halfway down the hill, Eddie was sliding over the pony's shoulders. It just ran faster, and with a sickening sense of impending doom, Eddie felt himself falling over to one side. He managed to keep a leg over the pony, but the only thing he could think of to do was reach up around its neck and hold on for dear life.

There he was, traveling upside down at high speed over a coarse asphalt surface. Every time the pony took a step it would knee Eddie in the back, whappity-whap, whappity-whap! Eddie looked up into the foaming mouth and nostrils of his assassin and prayed for a miracle. His body was aching, his fingers were losing their grip. In a moment that felt like an eternity, Eddie finally had to let go. He hit the pavement doing forty miles an hour and started his long skid down the hill. That's when the pony decided to tap dance on his ribs. Instead of going around Eddie, the pony went right over him, leaving some lovely bruises in the shape of hoofprints.

When Eddie slowly picked what was left of himself up off the pavement, he realized that half of his prayer had been answered. He was still alive! Now he would just wait to see if the pony dropped dead in answer to the other half.

The boys got so fed up and beat up by the ponies they decided to get a horse. It was a small horse, mind you. Perhaps a bit too small, because it still thought and acted suspiciously like a pony. Its name was Ron. He was a beautiful small pinto horse with bold patches of color. In order to house him, the boys had to modify a pre-existing chicken coop, turning it into a small barn. They put a manger in one end and left room on the other end for a little wooden door, just big enough for Ron to pass under.

The boys took turns feeding and watering Ron. Feeding him was no problem; just give him a bat or two of hay and a half can of his favorite food, sweet feed. Watering him was another story. Because there was no running water at the house, or anywhere on the hilltop for that matter, the boys had to lead Ron around the hillside about a quarter of a mile to a place where there was a spring. After doing it a few times, it became quite a chore. The other big chore was scraping out the barn each week. The boys were too lazy to fling the manure far, so over time it stacked up around the barn to a depth of a foot or two.

One day, it was Eddie's turn to feed and water Ron. He ducked inside the narrow door and grabbed a bat of hay. Then he opened a feed sack and fished out a half a coffee can of sweet feed. Ron was crazy about that stuff. He forgot all about the hay and started rooting around in the feed box with delight. Eddie still had to take Ron out to the spring, and he didn't have all day to wait for Ron to relish his oats. He clipped a rope to Ron's halter and dragged him away from his feed. Ron went reluctantly, looking longingly back over his shoulder at the little barn.

After a few minutes they arrived at the water hole. Ron dropped his head to drink. While he was drinking, Eddie had an idea. He knew exactly where Ron wanted to go when he finished drinking...back to his feed box! There was no bridle and bit for Ron, but Eddie figured he didn't need one. That horse was going back to the barn, so why should Eddie walk back when he could ride?

Without waiting for Ron to finish drinking, Eddie threw his leg across his back and climbed aboard. He figured that when Ron had had enough to drink, he'd turn around and amble home. Wrong. As soon as Eddie let go of the lead rope, Ron jerked up his dripping head, spun on a dime, and lit out down the path as fast as he could go. He put his ears back, stretched out his neck, and thundered along the path sending clods of dirt flying into the brush. Eddie had never ridden so fast in his life! He was certain to be killed.

Thinking quickly, Eddie realized that when they reached the yard, there was a downhill stretch where Ron would probably slow down enough for Eddie to leap off. A broken leg would beat a broken neck. But, no. When Ron hit the yard he just ran faster.

Eddie looked up and saw the narrow gate leading into the barnyard. Ron always slowed to a walk when he passed through the gate. Eddie figured he'd jump for his life when Ron slowed down for the gate. But, no. When Ron hit the gate he just ran faster.

In the half second after Ron passed through the gate Eddie looked up and saw the tiny barn door, just big enough for Ron to pass under. He was sure that Ron would finally slow down to enter the barn and he could at last leap off. But no. Ron had only one thing on his mind...sweet feed! He hit the barn doing around ninety miles an hour and Eddie hit the barn wall over the door at the same speed. KERSPLAT! Ron slid out from under Eddie. Eddie sailed spectacularly off of Ron. He flailed his arms in the air as he fell spread eagle on his back. He could have been seriously hurt except for one thing...horse manure! Eddie landed KERSPLAT on a deep cushion of smelly horse manure. He waited while the stars stopped spinning, then he sat up and checked himself out. His arms worked, his legs seemed to work, his spine didn't appear to be broken. He breathed a sigh of relief, wiped some horse hockey from his face, and looked to heaven. With a smile of gratitude he thanked God for horse manure! He owed it his life.

Hawaii

Whenever ponies and horses weren't trying to permanently disable Eddie, his classmates in the dumb class were. Eddie's mom began to worry. Then she started to plan. She called her brother, E.K, who was a pilot for Northwest Orient Airlines. His route carried him from Chicago to Tokyo and back every couple of days. He had chosen to settle with his family halfway between, on the island of Oahu. Eddie's mom called to explain the situation and asked if it might be possible for him to come visit for a while...or a semester!

So it was that Eddie found himself saying goodbye to his family at the Greyhound bus station in Charleston, WV. It was a cold, grey afternoon in a dingy part of town, and Eddie, only thirteen-years-old, was stepping onto a bus that would take him through Cincinnati, Indianapolis, and on to Chicago where his uncle would meet him. He'd never traveled before; never been away from home. A lump came up in his throat, but he tried to swallow it down. Bravely he hugged his mom and dad. He punched his brothers on the shoulder and said goodbye.

"Hey, it beats the dumb class!" he said, trying to control the tremble in his voice. "I'll send you some postcards!"

By the grace of God, Eddie managed his transfers, didn't lose his luggage or get lost himself. When he stepped off the bus the next day, there was his Uncle E.K, waiting for him. They took a taxi through the busy streets of Chicago, Eddie craning his neck to look up at the skyscrapers. They stepped out of the taxi into dirty snow and entered a high-rise hotel. Eddie couldn't remember ever being in a skyscraper, much less spending the night.

The next morning they rode to the airport and boarded a huge jet. Uncle E.K. showed Eddie around the cockpit. Then he introduced him to a pretty stewardess who took him back to his seat and buckled him in. Eddie had never flown, except for the time he jumped off the roof, and he was a little worried. When the plane roared down the runway for takeoff, he shut his eyes and gripped his armrest so hard he was afraid he'd leave dents in it. Once the plane was airborne, the vibration settled down and Eddie got up the nerve to look out the window. The ground was so far below him it didn't look real. It looked like a model of a city, of towns, of farms. The sun glinted off the snowy fields and frozen lakes. It was beautiful.

After a couple of hours, the land ended and the ocean began. It was so blue it looked black. Little puffy clouds dotted it here and there. As the plane passed over one larger cloud, Eddie was surprised to see the plane's shadow surrounded by a circular rainbow. The flight went on and on, and the dry air made Eddie's throat burn. At last, he looked down on a green jewel in the indigo sea. It was the big island of Hawaii. Crowning the island were two volcanoes...real ones; Mauna Loa and Mauna Kea. Next they flew over the island of Maui with its own volcano, Haleakala. They began their descent over the slipper-shaped island of Molokai and Eddie's ears began to hurt. As they descended from their marathon flight, everything began to hurt; Eddie's backside ached, his eyes burned, and his ears felt like they were about to burst.

Finally, the plane touched down and rolled to a stop. The cabin door was opened, and in that moment a breath of humid, healing tropical air flowed inside. It smelled like exotic flowers and pineapple. It soothed Eddie's itching eyes and dry skin. He said to himself, "This is what Heaven will smell like!"

Eddie and Uncle E.K. got in a car and drove out of the colorful city of Honolulu under the shade of orange and scarlet Flamboyant trees. They wound up into the knife-edged mountains that divide the island and passed through the Pali tunnel. When they emerged from the dark into the brilliant sunshine on the other side, Eddie nearly lost his breath. There, stretched out before them, was Paradise: an aquamarine horizon that changed to robin's egg blue where it met the creamy shore, lush tropical forests running up steep volcanic slopes, flowers, butterflies, waterfalls and a rainbow.

Eddie greeted his aunt and two little cousins. They showed him were he'd sleep. The next morning they helped him enroll in his new school. It was a little different from West Virginia. The school was huge. The students wore island print shirts and no shoes. Eddie moved from one classroom to the next for his classes. Lunchtime was in an enormous dining hall, where on one occasion they served meatballs, rice balls, and apples; it was just too tempting. Before he knew it, Eddie was in the middle of a food fight. The room was divided by a central aisle, and in a moment meatballs were flying across it like the Battle of Bull Run. Eddie particularly enjoyed the way the milk cartons could be opened and thrown like wet hand grenades. The vice principal jumped on a table to try to stop the fight...bad idea! He instantly became the target of every projectile in the lunchroom.

For five months, Eddie tried to forget how homesick he was by losing himself in the adventure of Hawaii. He snorkeled in an extinct crater, hiked across lava fields, and tried to surf. He was fascinated by the "Toilet Bowl," a lava tube connected to the sea that filled and flushed every time a wave came in. He enjoyed a waterski show at the Navy Base at Kane Ohe Bay. At the end, a man was pulled into the air on a large kite and circled the bay. Just as he was coming down, two fins sliced the water in front of him; man-eating hammerhead sharks! He had just enough altitude to pull his knees to his chest, sail over them, and glide onto the dock. He was lucky. Eddie's uncle told him of some other soldiers who weren't. They bought a box of steaks from the military store and a box of hand grenades. They got hold of a rowboat and a couple of six-packs of beer and rowed out to the middle of the bay, a famous breeding ground for hammerhead sharks. After a few too many beers, they began to toss the steaks overboard. Once the sharks were in a feeding frenzy, the soldiers pulled out the hand grenades. The sharks were so crazy they would bite anything. One shark bit a hand grenade and charged into the side of the boat. Eddie could guess how that story ended.

Eddie was doing well in school but he was getting worried about a rumor going around about something called "Kill Haole Day." Haoles are foreigners that live in Hawaii, just like Eddie. Apparently, on Kill Haole Day, the Hawaiian kids would kill the foreigners, or at least beat them up. It reminded Eddie of the dumb class! Fortunately, the day came and went, and Eddie was perfectly fine. In fact, he kept on being fine until he flew back to the States the following June, one week after the dumb class was let out for the summer!

Old Henry

Old Henry appeared at the back door late one afternoon. He looked like an ancient sailor, returning from the sea. His face was ruddy and lined with wrinkles; his hair, gray and uncombed. He wore an old pair of boots and carried the rest of his belongings in a faded duffel bag. He mumbled when he talked, because most of his teeth were missing, but as he looked up at Eddie's mom, standing on the back porch stairs, she pieced together that he was hungry and that he had a reason for being at their house.

As he sat at the table, soaking cornbread in his soup beans, his story began to come out.

"You seen them tombstones back of the house there?" he asked. "Them's my people. I's raised right here on this hilltop. I've been away for a while now, working here and there, tryin' to make a livin'. But now I'm back; I'm home. Wondered if there'd be anything I could put my hand to around here? I'd be much obliged."

Old Henry spent the night on the couch while Eddie's folks tried to figure out what to do with an old alcoholic with no place to go. In the morning, they invited him to stay on, hoping they'd figure something out.

What they learned was that Henry had been an old time logger. He was tougher than a hickory stump, but walked with a limp from an accident in the woods. As Eddie's dad talked to Henry, he began to get inspired. He invited Henry to walk the twenty-seven acres up behind the house. "Cruising" the timber, Henry spotted stands of poplar and oak that had grown up in the years since he'd had been away. The trees ran clear up to the ridge line, and they were ready to be harvested. He and Eddie's dad decided to go into business together.

The first investment was a sturdy, two-stall pole barn that went up back of the house. It was sided with pine boards, but the floor had to be of black gum because it will never split. When it was finished, Eddie's dad and Henry went off to the stock sale. When they came back, they were as proud as peacocks. They were followed by a man pulling a horse trailer. When the doors were opened, royalty stepped off the trailer; a matched pair of golden Percheron work horses that Henry named "Dick" and "Bess." They were amazing animals, their heads nearly reaching to the roof. Their backs were as broad as a couch, and white "horse-feathers" ruffled their enormous hooves.

The next day, Henry expertly harnessed them up, placing brown leather horse collars around their sturdy necks before putting on the metal hames. He threw the leather harness over their backs, adjusting straps here and there and fastening the crupper under their tails. He hooked the chains to a "single tree", a piece of wood that kept the chains spread and out from under their hoofs. The logs would be felled and hooked to the single tree for dragging down to the truck that waited in the holler.

With the proceeds from their first sale of logs, Eddie's dad bought a small metal building that he set up to be Henry's place up near where the gravestones were. Each day, Henry would hitch up the horses and head to the woods with a chainsaw. In the evening, he would come back down the hill, hang the harness on the wall and carefully comb out the golden coats of Dick and Bess. He'd stand back to admire his handiwork, throw his chest out, and proudly say, "Five thousand dollars wouldn't take them horses off this hill!" Then he'd retire to his little house with a six-pack of Budweiser, and we wouldn't see him until the next day.

Henry got to be part of the family, or we became part of his. One evening, the boys were shelling out peanuts from a large sack Eddie's mom had brought home. Henry got to hankerin' after some peanuts, but he had no teeth to chew them with. Looking around, he saw a coffee grinder sitting on the kitchen counter. His eyes squinted and the corners of his grizzled mouth went up. He'd show those young pups! He took a handful of peanuts and went to the grinder. Pouring them into the hopper, he began to crank the handle. He kept cranking and held his hand under the spout. He waited and waited. I'm not sure what he was expecting, but what finally came slowly out of the grinder was long and brown and looked too much like something you'd accidentally step in. Henry's smile faded, and with a snort, he flung open the back door and pitched his handful outside.

Henry stayed with the family all through one year and into the next. His health slowly began to get worse as his years of drinking finally caught up with him. About the time the timber was done, so was Henry. One afternoon, he hobbled down to Eddie's house. He warmed himself by the heater for a bit and then moved over to the couch. He didn't speak for a while and the boys figured he'd dozed off. When at last they looked over at him, they realized he'd drifted on into eternity, right there on their couch.

If you ever get a chance to visit that old farmhouse, and you walk up on the knoll behind it, you may see some old sandstone grave markers. Beside them is one that will be newer. It is a simple stone for a simple man. It bears the name "Henry." He's home.

The 'Possum Piggybank

Australia is full of mammals with pouches; kangaroos, wallabies, and wombats. They are known as marsupials. West Virginia is home to only one species of marsupial, the lowly 'possum. Possums have the distinction of being the only animal in the state with a pouch. They also have more teeth packed into their jaws than any other mammal. But their crowning feature has to be their homeliness. In nature's beauty pageant they come in dead last. They have wet pink noses, two beady little eyes, pink and black ears, and dirty grey fur. They drag a long, scaly tail behind them as they search for garbage or dead animals to eat. They also happen to be one of the dumbest animals in the forest.

Eddie and the boys had saved up their money and bought a Havahart trap. They'd seen it in the back of Boy's Life magazine. It was a rectangular box made of wire with a door on either end that caught animals alive. Inside was a moveable tray that held the bait. When an animal entered, it stepped on the pan, and the doors dropped.

The boys would go out into the woods, searching for likely looking spots and set their trap. They'd smear some peanut butter on the pan and prop the doors open. Then, they'd return home to wait. In the morning, they'd race out to the trap, hoping to find some exotic wildlife. Most of the time the trap would be empty, but the times it did hold something, it was usually a 'possum.

"Hey! We got something!"

"Ahhh, just another ol' 'possum..."

Then a plan began a formulatin' in Eddie's mind. What if they tried to tame one? He'd heard the old boast about folks living so far back in the holler they used 'possums for house cats. What if they could really do it?

So, they carried the trap to the barn and gathered around as Eddie slowly opened the back door and gingerly grabbed the disgusting tail. He figured the head, with its fifty teeth, was still inside the cage. While Scotty and Jimmy held one end of the cage, Eddie slowly extracted the 'possum. It didn't want to come out. It held on to the pan, the sides, the door before finally letting go. When it did, it swung back and came a hair of grabbing Eddie by the britchie leg, but he quickly hoisted it out of range.

The 'possum, being a marsupial, has a special tail. Besides being very ugly, it is also "prehensile", which means it can grab a limb with it and hang upside down. Truth is, 'possums will often sleep hanging upside down, so this particular 'possum wasn't too worried as it hung there. It tried once or twice to twist around and climb up its own body so it could sink some of its teeth into Eddie's wrist, but he managed to shake it back down. After a few minutes, it relaxed, and so did Eddie!

The boys gathered around and one after another began to reach out and touch their 'possum, just momentarily at first and always on the side away from the teeth. The 'possum jumped nervously the first few times, but after a while it seemed to understand they meant it no harm and settled down. Within a half hour, the boys were petting it's back without fear. They carried it to the back porch of the house where they kept an old refrigerator carcass laid on its side for moments like these. They dropped their 'possum inside and covered the top with mesh wire. As they gazed on their new pet, it began to undergo a mysterious transformation. Maybe it wasn't quite as ugly as they'd first thought. Its fur began to look a bit more silver to them than gray. Its eyes looked more like ebony beads. Its little pink nose matched its pink ears. And that tail...we'll maybe it would clean up with some of Mom's dishwashing soap, once they tamed it a bit more.

In time, that 'possum was just as used to the boys as they were to it. It would let them pick it up and carry it around. They did manage to wash its tail, which was only a limited success. It was still pretty hideous, but while washing its tail, they discovered that their 'possum was a "she." How did they know? Because "she" had a pouch. Only female 'possums have pouches; they use them to carry their babies around.

How convenient to have a pet with a pouch! One day the boys decided to play a trick on their friends in Racine. They tucked a couple of quarters into the 'possum's pouch and trooped out the door. They hiked the dirt road into town, crossed the train tracks and the steel bridge, and arrived at the gas station, where there was a pop machine. As luck would have it, their friends, Ricky and Bud, were hanging around the gas station.

"Hey, what's that thing?" asked Ricky.

"Yeah, does it bite?" added Bud.

"Oh, this? This is our pet 'possum. You know, we live so far back up the holler we use 'em for house cats," replied Jimmy nonchalantly.

"Hmmm," said Ricky. "Are they any good?"

"Oh, yeah," said Eddie. "They're great. Here, let me show you..." With that he turned the 'possum upside down and shook her. Two quarters fell from her pouch, and without missing a beat, Eddie inserted them into the pop machine.

There was a stunned silence for a moment. Ricky looked at Bud. Bud looked at Ricky. Then, together they said, "Dang! I gotta get me one of them thangs !"

Eddie took a swig from the icy bottle and passed it to his brothers; along with a wink!

The T. V. Gets Tossed

Do you remember that Eddie's mother wasn't a big fan of T.V? One day, when she took the boys to town, they got to poking through the junk at a rummage sale. Under a large pile of this and that, they uncovered a small, twelve-inch T.V. set. The man in charge said it didn't work, so he let them have it cheap. Between them they came up with two dollars and walked out of there with an investment. Their mother withheld judgment for the time being.

A few days later, they took it to an appliance repair store and were thrilled to learn that it only need a fifty-cent tube to make it work. "Work" was a word open to some interpretation. When they got it home, it only got one channel, and that looked like it was being broadcast from the North Pole because of all the snow on the screen. In time, the boys found that the best reception could be gotten out on the upstairs front porch. The picture improved even more if one of them would stand beside it and hold onto the antenna. After a few hours, little Gray got tired of antenna duty, and quit. Greg thought up the idea of unrolling a few feet of aluminum foil, connecting it to the antenna, and suspending the rest from the railing. It didn't work as well as Gray, but the boys thought he needed a break.

Bit by bit the electric glow of the T.V. lured Eddie and the boys from their adventures. They spent more and more time with their chins propped in their hands watching one show after another. It all came to a head one Saturday evening.

"Love, American Style" was a popular show at the time, pushing the limits of what was socially acceptable. Racy skits were populated by girls prancing around in skimpy bikinis. It was a whole new world for a bunch of boys who didn't even have a sister! That evening, as they were stewing in their hormones, their mother happened to walk up the steps to the porch to see what they were doing. There were her sons, glued to the T.V, their minds turning to Jello. But what were they watching? She was horrified! It was indecent! They were being corrupted, and she wasn't going to stand by quietly and watch it happen.

Her eyes narrowed, she bit her lower lip, and she marched to the T.V. She lifted it from its altar and yanked the cord from the wall. Speechlessly, Eddie and the boys followed her with their eyes as she turned and headed down the steps. She stormed out the door and marched to the edge of the yard. With a mighty heave, she tossed it over the hill where it fetched up twenty feet away under a Multiflora rose bush.

Eddie's mother never cussed, and that evening was no exception. She didn't need to. As the boys looked longingly over the hill, their mother turned to face them with prophetic fury. The fire that flashed from her eyes couldn't have been more dramatic if it had fallen from Heaven. They squirmed before her moral outrage.

"I have done my best to raise you boys. I've taken you to church every Sunday, and I've tried to teach you right from wrong. But listen to me and listen to me good. If you're going to watch anything like that again, IT WILL BE OVER MY DEAD BODY!"

That was the last time Eddie or the boys ever watched T.V. at home.

Go Play Outside

Now that the T.V. was gone, the boys decided to follow their mother's advice, "Go play outside!" One afternoon his brothers ran inside to invite Eddie to come out an play a special game they'd prepared, "Cowboy and Indians."

"Isn't that supposed to be "Cowboys and Indians?" Eddie asked.

"Not this time. You're going to be the cowboy, and we're going to be the Indians."

When he asked how to play, they led him outside to the edge of the yard and carefully tied him to a young sassafras tree. Then, when he was secured, they began to pile brushwood up around his feet. When it got to the height of his knees, they produced a box of matches and commenced lighting the fire. As the smoke started to rise, Eddie's brothers ran off laughing. Eddie began to holler.

Fortunately, his mother was standing at the kitchen sink, doing dishes. She had a good view of the back yard, and was used to keeping vigil over her cubs from that vantage point. At that moment, she spotted a low cloud of smoke drifting across the yard. A second later, she heard Eddie shriek. Drying her hands, she stepped out the back door to see what was going on. There was her first born, tied to a burning stake, and from somewhere behind the bushes she could clearly make out the sound of stifled giggles. As she untied the knots, Eddie looked up into his mother's face. They may have had their differences at times, but at that moment, she was his favorite person in the world!

Eddie and the boys were always building something in the backyard. One time, for their father's birthday, they selected a young locust tree and nearly killed themselves hoisting a two-hundred pound purple martin house to the fragile branches in the top.

Another time, they went into the woods and cut down twenty-foot saplings. They dragged them back to the yard and practice the lashing they'd learned in the Boy Scouts. They formed enormous tripods that looked disturbingly similar to illustrations from the War of the Worlds and left them dotted around the yard.

One of their best creations was a huge rope swing suspended from an old apple tree on the hillside out back. The rope was a good twenty feet long with a piece of wood tied to the bottom to make a seat. They tried all variations of pushing and running with the swing to gain more altitude, but they found that tying a secondary rope halfway up the main rope produced effects worthy of a theme park. As the swinger was sailing forward, out over the void, the puller would haul back on the control rope causing the swinger to soar skyward, with his feet aiming toward the clouds. The altitude reached was breathtaking.

During their time at Racine, Eddie's folks must have decided life was too tame, because they brought home a couple of foster brothers. They hadn't really planned on it. They'd been down to the jail to visit an acquaintance of Eddie's dad and happened to see two kids sitting behind bars.

"What did they do?" asked Eddie's mom.

"Oh, nothing. Their folks are in jail for fighting, and we ain't got no place to keep the kids."

"I'll take them," said Eddie's mom without hesitation.

And so, Eddie wound up with two more brothers, Perry and Ore. Ore was in high school, smoked, and was so good looking he had to fight the girls off him. Perry was his little brother. He was about eleven years old. He had big brown eyes and long hair. He had perfected the art of annoying his big brother, and he turned his talent on Eddie and his brothers in short order.

One day, Perry was riding the swing and Eddie was pushing. Perry was making comments about how weak Eddie was, how ugly he was, how useless he was, how dumb he was... and Eddie was getting a little tired of it. He looked at Perry, swinging away on the rope, then he looked at the control rope he held in his hand. An evil thought came into his head, and he didn't fight it hard. He jerked back on that rope, and Perry nearly did a back flip out of the swing. When Perry sailed out the next time, Eddie pulled harder. Perry's was going higher and higher. His feet were nearly hitting the top limbs of the apple tree. He began to get scared and told Eddie he wanted down. Eddie wasn't in the mood to let Perry down. He pulled harder, and Perry began to beg.

"Aw, be quiet you little chicken," said Eddie.

"LET ME DOWN!", screamed Perry. "I'm gonna fall!"

"You aren't going to fall," Eddie said with exasperation.

Then Perry fell. It was spectacular. As he sailed out into the blue, he sort of came disconnected from the swing. He flapped his arms like a young buzzard. He turned a slow somersault in the air. Then he hit the ground with a sickening thud. Eddie just stood and stared.

"OOOhhh! My arms!" moaned Perry. Eddie breathed a sigh of relief. At least Perry was still alive. Eddie ran down the hill. He'd recovered enough to think of a sarcastic remark, but just as he was going to make it, he looked down at Perry. Both his arms looked like backward Z's. It made Eddie feel queasy; he didn't want to think what it made Perry feel like. Suddenly, he became very concerned and felt horribly guilty. He gently helped Perry to his feet and led him toward the house. Coming through the back door, Eddie bumped into his mom who was talking on the phone.

"Mom! Mom! Perry's broken his arms." Eddie gasped.

His mother put her hand over the phone and glanced at Perry. He seemed to be conscious and breathing. "Put him over there on the couch," she said. "I'll get to him when I get off the phone."

Eddie felt a mixture of emotions. On one hand, his own conscience was hurting him just a little less than Perry's arms. On the other hand, he had to admire his mother's cool, collected attitude. He wondered sometimes if ice water didn't run in her veins.

Perry came back from the hospital with two shiny white casts. He didn't do much swinging after that.

One afternoon some old golf clubs showed up at the house, and the boys began to practice for the Masters. They'd hit those balls all over the weedy back yard. Sometimes, a ball would fly further and disappear over the hill. Thus it was that Eddie found himself slashing through the weeds as he ranged over the hillside looking for his golf ball. On one circuit, as he was coming up the hill, he came up on an old tree stump. Perched on that stump was an enormous copperhead snake, coiled and ready to strike. Eddie jumped back but didn't panic. He looked around for a weapon. All of a sudden, he looked down and saw he had a shining nine iron in his hand. What a coincidence! The copperhead was teed up perfectly. Eddie took his stance. Wiggled his butt once or twice, like the pros, and hollered, "Fore!" The nine iron arced gracefully through the air and the head of the snake sailed fifty yards through the air before landing right beside the imaginary 18th hole.

One afternoon a friend of Eddie's father climbed the hill on his big Honda 650 motorcycle. While the men were inside talking, Eddie and the boys lovingly looked over every inch of the shiny red bike. What a machine! Finally, Eddie got up the nerve to go inside and ask permission to ride it. "No problem," said his dad's friend and tossed him the key. Eddie trembled with excitement.

Outside, however, it was a different matter. Eddie had never ridden a motorcycle before. He'd never operated a machine that had a clutch either. When he tried to start the bike, it stalled. He tried again. It stalled again.

"Give it more gas," his brothers urged.

So Eddie opened her wide up and popped the clutch. In a heart-swallowing second, dirt flew backwards and the front wheel lifted off the ground. Eddie hung on for dear life. Just as soon as he was able to get his balance he looked up to see the sawdust pile right ahead of him. There was no time to swerve, and the accelerator was still wide open. He hit the sawdust and sailed ten feet through the air. When he landed, he bounced once and went over sideways into the tomato patch. The heavy bike was sitting on his leg and the manifold was red hot. Eddie, struggling to keep it off his leg, was unable to release the accelerator, and the back tire was chewing through tomatoes like there was no tomorrow.

When he was finally rescued, Eddie hobbled inside and sat down. Maybe he'd wait until he got bigger or found a smaller motorcycle before trying to ride again.

A Cold Night on the Devil's Tea Table

Eddie always enjoyed telling about his exploits at school. Of course no one believed him, but that didn't slow him down for a minute. One adventure that captured his imagination was spending the night in unusual places.

One winter, there was a big snowfall. It was a wonderful dense snow that packed easily, and before they knew it, the boys had rolled several very large snowballs in the back yard. It didn't take much to find a way to roll them together in a circle. Then, with a shovel, they chopped the inside half off and with a heave, lifted each piece into the slot between two lower snowballs. They rolled more giant snowballs, and by carefully cutting, placing, and packing, they formed a large white dome. Next, they created an entry tunnel out of snow and...voila! A respectable igloo.

Eddie just had to spend the night in it, so he laid down some cardboard on the floor. He grabbed the old, brown sleeping bag and headed out for the night. It turned out to be a very loooong night. When he dragged himself in the house the next morning, his brothers asked, "So, how did you sleep?" Eddie shook his head but smiled, "I don't know about sleep, but I DID spend the night in an igloo!"

The day came when the old back porch finally gave up the ghost and had to be torn down. Eddie and his brothers knew practically nothing about construction, but they were geniuses when it came to demolition! In no time, the porch was just an uninteresting heap of half rotten boards. What they discovered under the porch was another story! They'd uncovered a six-foot square wooden covering that begged to be lifted. When they pried it up, they found themselves looking down the wide shaft of a shallow well. At the bottom, they could see rocks and litter standing in about six inches of water.

Eddie's imagination kicked into high gear. How many people could say they had spent the night at the bottom of a well? So, without wasting time, he grabbed the old ladder and lowered it to the bottom of the well. It wasn't a deep well, so he was able to dangle his foot over the side and reach the first rung of the ladder. He tossed a bucket down and descended. Before long, buckets full of stagnant water were being slung up out of the well. Of course, half of each stinky bucket dropped back down on Eddie, but he didn't care. He was motivated!

In time, the well was almost dry. When Eddie dragged himself back to the surface, he admired his work. After catching his breath for a few minutes, he looked over the pile of old boards standing to the side and selected several to drop into the hole to form a base. Then he jogged to the barn for a bale of hay. Once he broke that up and sprinkled it over the boards, he smiled to himself. He'd spend the night on a comfortable nest.

What he didn't count on was geometry. The diameter of the well was just at five and a half feet. Eddie's feet stuck out about three inches further, only in a well there is no "further." For the first few minutes of the evening, he curled up happily on his trusty sleeping bag. Then he felt cramped and needed to stretch, but when he tried to extend his legs they banged into the wall. Oh, well, he'd just turn over. That worked for a few more minutes until he again felt the need to stretch. Bang! Right back into the wall.

He flipped one way...he flipped the other. He lay on his back and put his feet in the air. He stood up and paced in a circle. He lay back down. He looked at his watch.

The next morning his brothers asked, "So, how did you sleep?" Eddie shook his head and tried to manage a smile. "I don't know about sleep, but I DID spend the night in a well."

It was the dead of winter, and bitterly cold. Eddie and Jimmy came up with an idea. EVERYBODY goes camping in the summertime. But how many people go camping in the winter? Not many. Only rugged individuals, real "he-men" like Eddie and Jimmy would dare to attempt it.

So they threw together their gear and headed up the side of the mountain. Their destination was known as the Devil's Tea Table, a giant sandstone feature that rose above the ridge line, all that was left after the surrounding stone had eroded. It was famous for the rattlesnakes that crawled around it during the Dog Days of summer, but there'd be no snakes in January. Perfect!

As Eddie and Jimmy trudged up the mountainside under their load of gear, they were followed by their three faithful dogs; Caspian, Glory, and Fang. Caspian, the largest of the three was an enormous dog that looked like a mangy cross between a wolf and a German Shepherd. He was a noble beast though, who'd submitted without complaint to being dosed with "Happy Jack", a foul smelling treatment for mange. It had halfway worked.

Glory was a happy soul, a yellow beagle-like female that loved to hunt. She followed the boys everywhere, with a cheerful dog smile on her face, ready for whatever came.

Fang was another story. The boy's grandmother owned a petite, long-haired Chihuahua named Princess. When Princess gave birth, the boy's grandmother insisted on giving one of the tiny puppies to her grandsons. The puppy, a big-eyed, big eared trinket, suitable for the lap of some high society matron, was met with scorn when she first set foot on the hill.

"What in the world is THAT?" cried the boys.

"Get a flyswatter and kill it," they said.

The pup just stood her ground and stared at the boys as if to say, "You talkin' to me?"

After a few minutes, Eddie said, "Well, it can't be helped. That puppy's not to blame for her genetics. But if she's gonna stay on this hill, she needs a name to make up for her size." In the end, the boys settled on the name, Fang.

It didn't take them long to realized they'd chosen a good name. Ounce for ounce, Fang was the toughest dog on the hill. She was the epitome of the old hillbilly saying, "It ain't the size of the dog in the fight. It's the size of fight in the dog!" Fang would bully the other dogs away from the food dish so she could eat first. She would chase strangers off the hill. She barked furiously at the family cow, nipping at its heels as it ran for its life.

When Eddie and Jimmy reached the ridge, the sun was going down. A cold day was turning into a frigid night. They rolled their sleeping bags out on the relatively flat slab of the Tea Table and lit a small fire. They cooked a couple of weenies and heated some beans. Then they turned in for the night.

That slab of stone wasn't only hard as a rock, it was ice cold! After a miserable hour, Eddie turned to Jimmy and said, "You sleepin'?"

"Nope," said Jimmy.

"Wanna zip our sleeping bags together so we can trap some heat?"

That's what they did. The problem was...there wasn't much heat to trap, and the cold kept getting colder. They tossed and turned, and turned and tossed. They stared up through the bare branches at an amazing star-filled sky. At one point, a large meteor flared noiselessly across the sky, so close the boys felt they could have been singed. But it didn't get them any warmer.

At last Eddie came up with an idea.

"Hey, Jimmy...What do you say we put those dogs in here?

By that point, Jimmy was ready for anything. And so were the dogs. They didn't need to be invited twice, and in no time were curled around the boy's feet sleeping like...well, dogs!

In the morning, Eddie and Jimmy climbed stiffly out of their sleeping bags followed by the hounds. Fang's eyes sparkled and she looked like she would crow if she were a rooster. Glory glanced around with her happy smile as if to ask, "Now what?" Jack just flopped his mangy rear down and had a thorough morning scratch, thumping the ground with pleasure.

Eddie and Jimmy looked at the dogs and just shook their heads. They decided to skip breakfast. They just wanted to get down the hill and into a warm house as soon as possible. When they walked in the door, they were greeted by their brothers.

"Hey, guys," they said. "How'd you sleep?"

Without even attempting a smile, they answered, "We didn't. BUT WE SPENT THE NIGHT ON THE DEVIL'S TEA TABLE!"

Squirrel Huntin'

Because Greg and Gray were born in the shadow of their big brothers, they had to grow up fast and tough. Gray was built solid, like a fireplug. He was a 'rassler. Greg was about the same size as his little brother, but his big brothers bragged that he was "wiry." He was a fighter. Together, they were a force of nature and easily stood up for themselves against their older brothers, or anyone else for that matter!

One day at school a fifth grade bully mistakenly made a comment about their mother. He was creative in the way he said it. Instead of calling her a word for a disreputable woman, he emphasized his point by calling her a "couple of #@^%&s."

Greg was in the third grade, Gray in the first. They hadn't had time to learn too much yet at school, but one thing they DID know. Nobody says anything about your momma!

Greg sailed into the boy, nearly twice his height, and knocked the wind out of him. Just as the bully recovered enough to grab Greg, Gray came at him, running. He didn't slow down when he hit the bully, he just kept going...right up his chest. He grabbed the kid around the head and kicked over backwards. The bully went flying sideways and landed on the ground; then Greg landed on him. Before the teacher pulled them off, they were satisfied that they'd successfully defended their mother's honor.

Another time, Greg and Gray announced they were going squirrel hunting. Their older brothers, who occasionally underestimated them, scoffed and asked, "With what?"

"Don't worry about it," they said. "You'll see when we come home with a bunch of squirrels!"

Greg, who would have been about nine at the time, whistled for his dog, Glory, and headed off the hill with his little brother. They hiked the mile around the hillside. Instead of crossing the river at Racine, they followed the road around to the mouth of Indian Creek. As they walked, they kept a sharp lookout for squirrels.

Sure enough, after about a half-mile they spotted a fat gray squirrel perched in the fork of a hickory tree. Glory commenced barking and leaping against the trunk of the tree. Gray looked at Greg and asked, "Now what?"

"We're gonna rock the snot out of that squirrel," said Greg. Of all the boys, Greg was the deadliest with a rock. He had a remarkable aim that made him the best basketball shot of the family and the only brother to play pitcher in baseball. Gray followed his example in picking up a handful of rocks and, together, they began to bombard the squirrel. Although it dodged behind the trunk and tried to hide among the leaves, it may just as well have shinnied down the tree and offered itself up peacefully. As it was, a rock caught it when it wasn't looking and knocked it from its perch. Glory took care of the rest.

"That's one," said Gray. "Let's go for some more."

The boys ambled along the road with their trophy hanging from their belt, constantly scanning the trees. At last, they spotted another, but it got away. Later on they saw another, but it managed to escape as well. Finally, they cornered one in a smaller tree that had no place to hide. Another well-aimed rock brought it down and Glory finished it off. Greg and Gray looked at one another.

"Well, that's one for you and one for me," said Greg. "You reckon we outta be headin' home?"

After a long, dusty walk, Greg and Gray entered the house. Their older brothers looked up from a puzzle they were working on. Eddie sniggered.

"Any luck?" he asked sarcastically.

"Yeah," chimed in Jimmy and Scotty. "Did you get anything?" they said, trying to hold back a laugh.

With that, Greg plunked two fat squirrels on the table. He looked at Gray and then at his big brothers. With a twitch in his jaw and a Clint Eastwood glint in his eye, he said, "Yeah. I reckon we did."

"Ugly Boys Gotta Go to School Today"

There are lots of kids that don't really like to go to school. Eddie and the boys had their own reasons. First, it was a mile hike to the bus stop. Second, the kids at school were mean. Third, the thermometer was hovering around zero that winter morning. Fourth, Perry, their foster brother, was rubbing it in because he didn't have to go.

Because Perry was only there temporarily, or so they thought, he hadn't been enrolled in school right away. Instead, he'd sit around the house all day while the boys were away at school, thinking of ways to be aggravating. This particular morning, he was prancing around the house chanting, "Ugly boys gotta go to school today. Pretty boys stay home! Ugly boys gotta go to school today. Pretty boys stay home!" It made Eddie so mad he wanted to do something to Perry that would make him not so pretty.

"Mom, it's freezing outside," the boys complained. Looking past the frozen nail heads on the dining room wall and out the window at about a foot of snow, they begged to stay home.

At that moment their father stepped out of his bedroom. He had always been a proponent of hardy living. He was accustomed to roughing it. Surely, his sons weren't concerned about a little cold weather!

"What are you boys talking about?" he asked. He looked out the window. "You call THAT cold? Why, a little snow's nothing to be afraid of. Here, let me show you."

And with that, their father skinned right down to his birthday suit. In a second he was out the back door. The boys looked out the window in bewilderment as they watched their dad race around the house, naked as a jaybird. He'd occasionally fling some snow in the air or fire off a snowball at the house. On the third lap, just before he came back inside, he lay down in the deepest snow bank of all and whooped as he made a snow angel.

The most amazing part of it was the way he nonchalantly walked back in the house and slipped on his robe as if nothing had happened. The boys stood staring, speechless. Then, they heaved a sigh and gathered their schoolbooks. After a demonstration like that, what could they say? They headed out the door to school.

Skinny Dippin"

When summertime rolled around, the boys headed to the river. Sometimes they'd take a bar of soap, sometimes not. They'd walk down the steep path until they got to the railroad tracks. Their neighbors, Red and Clotine, lived in a neat little clapboard house between the tracks and the river. On weekends, they were bad to drink and would get into fights that sounded like they were killing each other. The boys, trying to sleep on the upstairs front porch Saturday nights, were convinced they'd find a couple of dead bodies down the hill the next morning. But as they trotted past their house on hot cross ties, Red and Clotine would wave amiably, as if nothing had ever happened.

A hundred yards down the tracks, the boys dropped over the bank into high weeds. Elderberry bushes with clusters of tiny black berries grew thickly in the rich bottomland. Tall, purple-stalked Pokeberry plants crowded the path. When they were small, you could make "Poke Sallat" from the greens. As they got older, they produced clusters of intensely purple berries with a juice that would leave a neon stain. They were great for berry fights. Hairy poison ivy vines climbed the water birch trees. Eddie was particularly allergic to poison ivy. He'd had it on his hands and in his eyes. He even got it in his mouth one time. But the worst time was when he was out in the woods one day without any toilet paper. He carefully checked the leaves he used to wipe himself, but not carefully enough! The other kids in his class wondered why he kept squirming around on his seat all day.

At the river's edge the sandy bank dropped eight feet to the water. The river itself was only about two feet deep at this point and nearly fifty feet wide. The green water flowed over a yellow sandy bottom mottled with black flecks of coal. There was no one else around, and since they were all boys, Eddie and his brothers slipped off their shorts and draped them on a tree limb that hung out over the water. Then they raced, laughing and splashing, into the cool water.

There was lots of fun to be had at the river. They dug mud out of the banks and slathered it onto the steep sides. One after another they'd take turns sliding down until they had a wallowed out a mudslide. They covered their entire bodies in that same blue-grey mud and pretend to be aborigines. They climbed out on tree trunks leaning over the water and dared each other to jump. They explored the deep, eerie holes washed under fallen trees by the current.

One time, the boys heard a tragic story of a baby that had been drowned near a town three miles upstream. A few days later, Jimmy was exploring the deep water around a tree snag and burst to the surface, horrified.

"Eddie!" he yelled. "Get over here! I think I found that baby!"

Eddie borrowed the goggles, took a deep breath, and went below. Thick branches strained the blue-green water. A rock bass scooted for cover. He could just make out something trapped in the tangle below him. Gathering all his courage, he got closer and made out a small arm and a hand with tiny fingers. He reached out and took hold of it, then he kicked for the surface. When he burst to the top, he held the baby aloft. His brothers screamed and fled in all directions while Eddie laughed until he nearly cried. It was a doll baby.

One day, as the sun was going down, the boys headed to the bank. They reached for their shorts. Eddie and Scotty found theirs. So did Greg and Gray. But Jimmy's shorts were nowhere to be seen. Jimmy looked suspiciously at Eddie, but he swore he had nothing to do with it. Maybe, as the boys were jumping off that limb, Jimmy's shorts had fallen into the river and floated down to Racine? But, hey! Not to worry. They'd come up with some kind of idea.

In no time, the boys gathered a good supply of leaves off the pokeberry plants. They found a piece of vine that would serve as a belt. Before Jimmy knew it, they'd rigged him up with a pokeberry hula skirt. He was still strongly suspicious and said from under lowered eyebrows, "You just better hope Clotine isn't out in the yard!"

The boys jogged up the path through the elderberry bushes and climbed to the railroad tracks. They hot-footed it along the cross-ties. Just as they thought they were home safe, they heard the sound of laughter behind them. There stood Clotine, fit to be tied and laughing like a hyena.

"Mighty cute outfit ya got there, Jimmy" she said between guffaws. "Oughtta get me one a them!" Jimmy just picked up his pace and started planning his revenge.

A week later the boys were back at the river. When it was time to go, Eddie didn't notice his younger brothers had headed back ahead of him. He didn't pay attention to the treasonous snickers coming from the bank. When he finally climbed out of the water, his brothers were gone. So were his shorts!

He looked around desperately. It would be impossible to make another hula skirt by himself. He was furious with his brothers. He wanted to teach them a lesson. Just then, he stumbled across something half covered in mud. It was an old, rotten pair of shorts someone had left on the bank months ago. They were falling apart and covered with ants, but Eddie didn't care. The zipper didn't work, but that didn't matter either. What counted most at this moment was speed.

Eddie wiggled himself into the disgusting shorts, being careful not to tear them more than they already were, and raced up the path. He flew down the tracks, and if Clotine was out in her yard, he didn't even notice. With his sides heaving, he pulled himself up the shortcut, ignoring the scratches of blackberry vines. He just wanted to get to the house before his brothers.

So it was that when his brothers came tumbling in the backdoor, still laughing at the prank they'd played on their big brother, they froze in their tracks. There sat Eddie at the dining room table, cool, calm, and collected.

"Hey, guys!" he said, as if nothing had happened.

"How...how did you get here?!?" they gasped.

"Oh, I've got my ways." said Eddie mysteriously. He'd let them wonder for a long while.

The Mighty Mud Cat

Christmas was coming and Eddie had drawn Gray's name. He wanted to give him the best present he'd ever gotten, so he started thinking hard. He didn't have much money, so the mini-bike got crossed off the list. A trip to Disney World was out too. Eddie was starting to get desperate. One day, as he was flipping through an old National Geographic, he came across an add for a Folboat, a folding kayak that you could build yourself...at home. Bingo!

Eddie couldn't afford the $149.95 it would take to buy a Folbot, but that didn't matter. He would draw up his own plans and build a boat from scratch. He was going to need some help with this project, so he went to his dad. Yes, he'd help buy the materials. Yes, they could put it together in his dad's office. Yes, he'd help when it came time to make the cuts. Eddie was thrilled!

A few weeks before Christmas, Eddie made a sign and hung it on the office door.

"Santa's Workshop. Stay out if you want to live to Christmas. This means you, Gray! Ho Ho Ho!"

The mystery grew. There was tiptoeing around at night. Sounds of heavy objects being dragged through house floated up to where Gray was trying to sleep.

There was the sound of sawing, rasping and sanding coming from behind the office door. Was that a power tool? What could be going on?

Poor little Gray. He was only eight years old, and the suspense was worse than anything he'd lived with in his short life. He just HAD to take a quick peek! He checked the dining room. No one was there. The living room was empty. So was the kitchen. He timidly said, "Anybody here?" No answer.

Gathering all his nerve, Gray tiptoed down the hall to the office. His hand went out to the doorknob. He slowly turned it and opened the door a crack. He stuck his head in just enough to see the bow of a home made john boat when all of a sudden...

"BAM!"

Someone grabbed him by the scruff of his neck and the seat of his britches, lifting him into the air. He heard Eddie's furious voice.

"You two-bit, four-flushin', wall'eyed, cock-a-mamie, jackanape! What do you think you're doing?!?"

With that, Eddie spun little Gray around and flung him the full length of the hallway. Gray hit the rough wooden floor and skidded over the splinters, but he didn't stop to lick his wounds, he was more interested in saving his life! He leapt to his feet, dashed around the corner, through the dining room, and into the living room here he sailed over the top of the sectional couch to go to earth in the tiny space left where the couch didn't quite reach the corner. He tried not to breathe as he trembled and prayed for deliverance.

Fortunately, Eddie didn't find him. By Christmas morning, all was forgotten, and Eddie led Gray down the hallway to the office. He tore off the sign and opened the door. There, covered in fresh paint, sat Gray's boat. It was a flat-bottomed riverboat with two seats. Across the bow was lettered the words "Mud Cat." Mud Cat's are a kind of catfish that live in the Big Coal River. They aren't very pretty to look at, but they're tough. In a way, they can be like brothers; sometimes the relationship can get a bit ugly, but brotherly love is tough and can overcome a multitude of sins!

That summer, there wasn't enough money for the family to go away on vacation. It was decided they'd pull a Huck Finn. The family would float down the Big Coal River in the Mighty Mud Cat to the place where it joined the Kanawha River below Charleston.

There was no way everyone would fit in Gray's boat, so Eddie's dad borrowed an aluminum johnboat from a friend. Eddie's mom bought bologna, marshmallows, and hot dogs. The boys rounded up fishing poles and the tent. Soon, it was time to push off!

The two boats nosed out into the calm water. It ran shallow over beds of sand at this point. Large water maples leaned out over the banks, throwing shade on the travelers. At spots along the way, trees had fallen over into the river and the current washed deeper holes from under them where red-eyes and catfish liked to hide. From time to time the boys would leap over the sides of the boat and splash through the shallows to climb onto the slanting trunks. There, they'd dive into the deeper water, cutting flips or doing cannon balls.

The family passed under the steel bridge at Racine and waved up to Ricky and Bud who were leaning over the railing. They jealously tossed a few rocks. The family approached a narrow section of the river that became rocky. The boys were in high spirits as they bounced off boulders and turned sideways in the eddies.

After a few hours, they came to a part of the river where there were no houses. They tied the boats off in the lee of a little island. While their mom unpacked supper, their dad began setting up a tarp in case it rained. The boys climbed through the brush to the head of the island and trotted back with driftwood for a campfire. Once night fell and they settled down for the evening, their dad stirred the fire and started in on one of his famous "Herbert Rabbit" stories. The family might have been poor, but life was good!

A couple of days later, they camped closer to a little town. Bill, one of the foster boys, invited Eddie to climb the bank with him and cross the bridge to a little store where he could resupply his chewing tobacco. On the way, he embarrassed Eddie by yelling at every girl, woman, and old lady, saying, "Hey, do you chew tobaccy?" While they were at the store, they ran into a raggedy looking kid who followed them back to their camp. He started talking to the boys and skipping rocks across the river. As it began to grow dark, he helped drag in some firewood. He wanted to spend the night. Eddie's eyebrows furrowed and he frowned. He thought about his family. He didn't want some stranger to hear about Herbert Rabbit! So he told the kid to go home. The kid didn't want to go home, but Eddie made him. It felt bad, but Eddie thought it was the right thing to do.

After five lazy days, the river widened and the current slowed. The boys could hear traffic in the distance, and coming around one last curve they saw a huge highway bridge spanning the river. Beyond the bridge, they could see the wide reaches of the Kanawha River and coal barges pushing their way upstream. They pulled the boats to the bank and tied them to a huge sycamore tree. Their dad climbed the bank to the highway and stuck out his thumb to hitchhike back to Racine for their car. The rest of the family had to wait.

While the slow hours went by, an elderly black gentleman appeared on the bank above them. He carried a five gallon bucket, three old Zebco 202 rod and reels, and a cooler. Behind him was his ancient father with a couple of camp stools and a formidable looking gaff hook. They were dressed in old clothes and obviously didn't have much money. They set up the stools in the shade of the sycamore and baited their hooks with putrid smelling dough balls.

The boys couldn't resist, and in no time they were squatting on the bank beside the two men.

"You all do much good, fishing here?" they asked.

"Oh, yes sir! We do all right!"

"What's that you're fishing with?

"This here's dough balls. We put a little bit of vanilla and peanut butter in 'em."

"The bass will bite that?"

"Oh, we ain't fishin' for bass. We after carp."

The boy's dad had once shared with them an old Scout recipe for cooking carp. You split a log in half and use wooden pegs to fasten the carp to it. You scoot it up close to the fire and let it cook. From time to time, you turn it so that it gets done through and through. When its just right, and the juices are running out, you pull out the pegs, throw the carp in the bushes, and eat the log!

All of a sudden, the old gentleman's rod tip began to move. He poised his hand above the handle and held his breath. One. Two. Three! He jerked back, like he was pulling the fish's eye teeth out. The pole doubled over and the man struggled to reel. Whatever it was, it was huge!

After a couple of minutes, the enormous scaly back of a three-foot carp broke the surface. The old man turned to his father with a grin and hollered,

"Get the gaff hook, Daddy! This here's our winter meat!"

When the leviathan was landed, he baited up with another dough ball and cast out into the still water. Ten minutes later he was hollering again,

"Wheee, oh! Get the gaff hook, Daddy! We got some more winter meat!"

It was a fitting end to our vacation. Like the old men, we didn't have much. We hadn't been able to go to the Smokies or the beach for our family vacation, but we made the most of what we had, and it turned out to be a great success!

"Hoooo-eee! Get the gaff hook, Daddy!"

Smokin'

Eddie and the boys weren't only fascinated with fire. They liked smoke too. One day their parents had to be away, so they were left with a babysitter. By this time, Eddie was a young teenager, and he was a little miffed that his parents didn't trust him to look after the tribe. After all, hadn't he proved his responsibility time after time? Hadn't he?

The babysitter came huffing up the hill and plopped into a chair. She looked around at the house and the boys. She asked about the bathroom. She considered asking for a raise before the job even began! As the morning progressed, though, she realized the job wasn't so bad. The boys were entertaining themselves and things seemed to be under control. In fact, she was beginning to get a little bored...and hungry. She looked around for something to heat up in the oven, but when she went to turn it on, she realized it wasn't like her oven at home. This was a gas oven. Not to be outdone, she looked around the kitchen and found a box of Ohio Blue Tip matches, the kind you can "strike anywhere."

She opened the door to the oven, turned on the gas...and the phone rang! She'd given the number to her boyfriend. Her face lit up with pleasure and she talked to him, trying to think of flirty things to say. As she talked, she wandered around the kitchen, pulling the long phone cord behind her. She giggled and looked out the window. She lowered her voice to share some secret with the boy. Finally, after a few minutes, she ran out of conversation and had to say goodbye. Because her ear had been pressed to the phone the whole time, she was unaware of the faint hiss of gas that had persisted throughout the call. She hung up and turned back to the oven. Innocently, she picked up the box of Ohio Blue Tips and pulled one out. She scratched it on the box.

"KAWHOOOOM!" The boys, sprawled out on the couch in the living room reading old National Geographics, felt the house shake. A couple of pictures fell off the wall. They leapt off the couch and dashed into the dining room. What they saw stunned them. There was the babysitter, dazed and upside down underneath the dining room table. Bits of smoke curled up from where her eyebrows had been. They followed her trail back into a kitchen that looked like a war zone. Chairs were overturned, pots lay on the floor, a smoky smell hung in the air.

"What happened?" they asked, after the babysitter recovered a bit.

"Well, I got this call from my boyfriend..." she began.

Eddie lifted an un-singed eyebrow and looked sagely at his brothers, "Boys, let that be a lesson to you. Love," he said knowingly, "can be a dangerous thing!"

A few weeks later, Eddie and the boys were sitting around that same dining room table. They were trying to think up something to do, but they were avoiding the word "bored" at all costs. That word was worse than a cuss word to their mother. If she ever heard them say they were bored, she'd find them something to do, usually chores!

Eddie's mom plopped down at the table and looked around. Her eyes fell on a pack of cigarettes a visitor had left the day before. She was a brilliant woman and more than a little sneaky.

"Hey," she said, casually picking up the pack of cigarettes. "You boys ever wonder what it'd be like to smoke a cigarette?"

Eddie looked at his brothers in bewilderment. Most mothers were threatening to skin their kids alive if they dared to smoke, and here was HIS mom, offering to light one up with them. He suspected something, but shrugged his shoulders and reached for a smoke. So did the other boys.

His mom fetched the Ohio Blue Tips from the kitchen and carefully lit each boy's cigarette. Then she lit her own and sat back to take a puff. One after another, each of her sons followed her example. They practiced holding the cigarette in different ways, trying to see who could look the coolest. They took tentative little puffs, not daring to deeply inhale. They worked on their flicking skills, trying to get the ash to fall in the ashtray. They weren't very disappointed when the cigarette finally burnt down to a smoldering stub, which they ground out in the ashtray. Their mother didn't say a word.

The next morning the boys woke up with a taste in their mouths like they'd spent the night licking out ashtrays. As hard as they brushed their teeth and rinsed their mouth, they could not get rid of the noxious flavor.

When they sat down at the breakfast table, their toast and eggs tasted like charcoal.

"I'm not sure what people see in smoking," was all their mother said. With that simple phrase, she'd taken all the rebellious fun out of sneaking behind her back to light up a cigarette. Eddie and his brothers knew when they'd been "had."

Eddie's mom wasn't the only sneaky one in the family. When it came to sneakiness, the apple didn't fall too far from the tree. Another foster brother came to live with them. His name was Bill. Bill was a mischievous twelve-year-old with a dimple and an infectious grin that could get him out of about anything. He also had a tobacco habit, but he didn't smoke. He either chewed Red Man tobacco or dipped Skoal snuff.

One day, Eddie and Bill were heading back to the house from Racine. They were walking along the hot railroad tracks, Bill masterfully spitting tobacco juice fifteen feet into the blackberry bushes along the right of way. Eddie, on a whim, asked for a chew. He knew the danger of swallowing the juice, so as he carefully tucked a small wad between his lip and gum, he made sure not to accidentally swallow the juice. Bill admired Eddie for taking a "chaw." Perhaps he could make something of him yet!

As they kept walking, Eddie began to get a bit cocky. "Hey, Bill" he said, "Wanna have a spit swallowing contest?" Now, there was no way in the world Eddie was going to really swallow the tobacco juice, he knew it would make him very sick. Instead, he planned to sneak-ily spit out his juice whenever Bill wasn't looking. Bill, on the other hand, had been chewing tobacco ever since he was knee-high to a grasshopper. He could swallow spit all day and not feel a thing!

"Bring it on!" he said with his famous grin. So they kept walking, stepping from one creosoted railroad tie to another, and NOT spitting (except when Bill had his head turned). Bill cheerfully prattled on, pointing out birds and looking at the clouds in the sky. Eddie started to get quieter. And then quieter. He began to feel a bit green around the gills. He was certain he'd been careful not to swallow any tobacco juice. What was going on?

As they climbed the hill to the house, it was all Eddie could do to keep his feet under him. Things began to spin and his knees wobbled. When they got to the yard, Eddie pitched over on the grass in the shade of the old apple tree. Everything began to go dark. He felt like he was looking up from the bottom of a deep well. Then he passed out.

When, at last, Eddie came to, there was Bill looking down at him. He had that famous smile going and the dimpled flashed. His blue eyes twinkled as he said, "Well, Eddie, I guess you lost!"

"I guess I did," moaned Eddie. He never tried tobacco again.

Ricky, the boys' friend from Racine, probably wished he'd never tried tobacco. One day, he decided to hike around the hillside to visit the boys. On the way out the door of his house, he grabbed a cigarette when his mother wasn't looking. He had a plan.

A half-mile around the hillside, there was an abandoned coal mine. It wasn't a commercial mine, just what they used to call a "house mine." It wasn't more than a three-foot high opening under a layer of sandstone where folks had dug out coal for their fireplaces. Eddie and the boys had poked their heads in before, but after crawling in a few feet, it sort of petered out.

Ricky had chosen this spot as the most secret and safe place he could imagine to smoke his cigarette. NO ONE would see him here! So, after checking to see if anybody was coming, he scrambled up the bank, through the greenbriar bushes and ducked into the opening. Once inside, he pulled out the slightly crumpled cigarette and fished for a match.

"KAWHOOOOM!" There was a flash and a roar, and the next thing Ricky knew, he was lying out on the road ten feet away. He hadn't counted on mine gas, a byproduct of the coal and a real hazard to miners in that area. When he struck the match, he ignited the gas. He had sailed like a cannonball out of the mouth of the mine. He picked himself up and felt around for broken bones. Everything seemed to be in order, though his face was stinging.

When Ricky finally came panting up the hill to the farmhouse, he was met in the yard by the boys. They weren't sure they recognized him, so they got closer.

"Ricky, is that you?"

"Sure is, why?"

"Well, your face is red as a beet and you haven't got any eyebrows!"

"Yeah, well, it's kind of hard to explain," said Ricky looking at the ground.

"Aw, you don't have to explain anything," said the boys. "We've seen this before...on our babysitter. You're in love, aren't you?"

Rat Fishin'

Mud. Mud everywhere. It was that time of year after the snow had stopped falling and before the sun really started to shine. It seemed like all it wanted to do was rain and rain some more. The sky was gray, the trees were bare, the ground was soggy. It was a hard time of year for a bunch of active boys.

But that didn't stop them from trying! They found an old softball one afternoon and headed to the back yard to play. Theirs wasn't much of a backyard. The flat ground had been taken up by a vegetable garden. An out-house sat in one corner. The hill with the tiny graveyard rose up behind that. Off to one side stood the pole barn for the workhorses. And every bit of it was covered with sloppy mud!

Greg was pitching, and Eddie got a piece of the ball. It sailed over the hill, landed with a soggy thump, and started rolling toward the barn. When they boys ran to fetch it, it couldn't be found.

"Get a flashlight from the house," ordered Eddie. "It's rolled up under the barn."

When a light had been produced, Eddie gingerly squatted down in the mud and aimed it into the dark netherworld below the barn floor. What he saw freaked him out. There, running back and forth in the darkness, were RATS! Dozens of rats. Big and small ones. It was a plague of Biblical proportions.

All thoughts of the softball disappeared at that moment, and Eddie's mental wheels began to spin. This presented an opportunity for good clean fun out of the rain and above the mud.

"Boys," he ordered, "forget the ball. Go in the house and get a fishing pole from the closet. Grab some cheese and come back as quick as you can."

It wasn't long before the boys were back with the pole and bait. They located a large knothole, flipped over some water buckets to sit on, and Eddie baited his hook with cheese. He lowered it carefully through the hole.

"You ever fish for rats before?" asked Greg suspiciously.

"Nope, but how hard can it be?" replied Eddie with false confidence. "You just wait for a bite and then jerk his eye teeth out!"

The boys huddled around, breathlessly intent on the rod tip, waiting for a bite. All of a sudden, the rod began to twitch. Eddie counted under his breath, "One, two...three..."

"WHAM!" Eddie jerked so hard he fell backwards off the water bucket. A shrill squeal pierced the air, followed by the adrenaline-inducing hum of line spooling off the reel. The boys leapt to their feet and began yelling encouragement. Eddie reeled and fought and sweated that rat in until it ran out of running room.

"THUNK!" There was a sound at the hole. When the boys bent over to look, they could see gray fur. A lot of it. The rat was huge! There was no way it was going to get through that knothole. Fortunately, the hole was at the edge of one of the floorboards. Eddie kept tension on the line and carefully maneuvered it to the crack between the boards over to where it widened out for one of the barn posts. As soon as there was clearance, Eddie pulled up hard and hoisted the rat into the air.

As he stared at the furious rat hanging from his line it began to dawn on him that he hadn't planned far enough ahead to know what to do with a rat if he actually managed to catch one. But here he was, and here IT was. Its squeals had attracted the attention of three or four hungry barn cats, and their eyes glittered as they stealthy began to approach. Eddie hoisted the rat higher in the air, worriedly looking at the cats. All of a sudden, two cats went for Eddie. In their frenzy to get at the rat, they began climbing Eddie's britchie legs, their claws going right through to the meat! He had to do something fast!

Eddie swung the rat in a circle over his head and in a mercifully quick moment, he smacked it against the barn wall, putting it out of its misery. It took a couple more moments to get the cats off Eddie and get him out of his misery. He sat shakily down on his water bucket, reeled in his line, and packed up the bait.

"Boys," he said, "That is how you go rat fishin'." They wisely declined to give it a go themselves. They also decided to let the rats keep their softball.

Chapter Four
High School, 1970-74, Age: 14-17

Total Anarchy!

Eddie and his brothers were making straight A's at school. They claimed it was because of all the National Geographics they read, but it may have had more to do with the school than the boys. At any rate, they were approaching high school age and their education was becoming an issue.

Eddie's dad was working as an area supervisor for a program called V.I.S.T.A, which stood for Volunteer In Service To America. It was a homegrown version of the Peace Corps, manned by longhaired college kids who wanted to help fight poverty. They were an interesting group of idealistic, left-wing radicals. They adopted Eddie and his brothers like they were family.

One of them, a guy named Dave, was the son of a math professor who taught at the prestigious Phillips Exeter Academy, an Ivy League boy's boarding school north of Boston. One day, as he was sitting around the dining room table with Eddie's parents, he asked about their plans for the boys' education.

"Have you ever thought of boarding school?" he asked.

"Why, we could never afford anything like that," said Eddie's mother.

"You'd be surprised," said Dave. "The school has a large endowment. If a student gets accepted, the school looks at his family's finances and pays whatever the family can't."

So it was that Eddie and Scotty found themselves in a classroom at a high school in Charleston, taking the Secondary School Admissions Test. A few weeks later they got a letter inviting them to New Hampshire for an interview at the Phillips Exeter Academy. How were they going to travel all the way from a hillside in West Virginia to the ivy-covered walls of New England? As it turned out, another VISTA volunteer, Chuck, was heading that way in his tiny Subaru hatchback. Eddie and Scotty squeezed themselves in and headed off on a long, hot road trip. They stopped along the way to camp out in the evenings, sweating and slapping mosquitoes.

When at last they reached the town of Exeter, New Hampshire, they went into culture shock. Students, dressed in coat and tie, were attending the summer session. As Eddie and Scotty were led around the campus, they stared up at the brick towers and classical Greek columns. They marveled at the athletic complex. They got lost in the library.

Toward the end of their visit, Eddie and Scotty were sitting on the curb out front of the admissions building.

On one side sat the admissions officer, on the other, one of the senior students. They'd been through all the formal interview questions, but on a whim, the admission officer turned to Eddie and asked, "So, Eddie, what's your political philosophy?" Most eighth graders would have had little to say, but Eddie had been hanging around with a vocal crowd of radical Marxists. Without batting an eye, he threw his fist in the air and shouted, "Total anarchy!"

The senior beside him nodded his head and said with a grin, "Cool!" To this day, Eddie is convinced that his answer got him into Exeter.

Down the Outhouse Hole

Eddie was awarded a full scholarship and arrived at Exeter with a suitcase full of old button-down shirts he'd gotten at Goodwill, a few ties, and a couple of slightly worn sports coats. He struggled with tying his tie, but he noticed that none of the other boys bothered with perfection either. They were mostly sons of politicians, investment bankers, and very successful businessmen. One of his classmates was the crown prince of Thailand!

Eddie was given a room on the third floor of one of the old brick dormitories. His roommate, David Abel, was Jewish boy from New York City. He talked about his trips to Europe and Christmas vacations in Colorado. David's uncle came to visit one weekend and took David and Eddie out to a fancy restaurant. Eddie had heard of lobster, but never seen, much less eaten, one! He relished each bite after carefully dipping it in melted butter. At about two-thirty that night, Eddie was bent over the toilet. The lobster had been too rich for him.

In fact, there was a lot about Exeter that was too rich for him, but he tried to make the best of it. As he sat in a neighboring dorm room, admiring the Persian carpet and listening to a description of what the boy's stereo was capable of, Eddie felt like he'd landed on another planet. And it wasn't just the things the boys talked about...it was the way they talked, "Pahk yah cah in Havahd Yahd." Everything felt alien.

Eddie missed his family very much. He realized he'd taken them for granted. He agonizingly marked the days left until Christmas vacation when the school would fly him home.

The Chuck Yeager Memorial airport at Charleston, WV, looks like something a daredevil test pilot might try to land on. Because there is very little flat land in West Virginia, the decision was made to chop the top off two mountains and dump them in the intervening valley. Eddie's knuckles turned white as he gripped the armrest during the descent. He reminded himself of the old pilot's adage, "Any landing you can walk away from is a good landing." He just hoped he'd be able to walk away from this one.

When he came through the gate, Eddie saw his family waiting for him. His mom hugged him and his dad took his suitcase. His brothers looked at him with wonder and admiration. They stuffed his bag in the old V.W. microbus and packed themselves in around him. Then the questions began to fly...

"Hey, Eddie, what's that place like?"

"Yeah, what all do you eat up there?"

"Did yuh meet any millionaires?"

The joy of being reunited with his family began to be replaced with astonishment. As he listened to his brothers talk, he came to the stark realization that they were a bunch of hicks. All his life, he'd grown up with these guys and never realized what a bunch of hillbillies they were. He was mortified!

Of course, his brothers weren't the ones who'd changed. Eddie had; he'd gone off to a high-fallutin' boarding school and he'd come home "uppity."

Now, God has his ways of dealing with pride, and Eddie stood in need of the treatment. When he finally climbed the hill to the old farmhouse, he also stood in need of a bathroom. But there WAS no bathroom, it was back to the old outhouse on that cool December afternoon. He dropped his suitcase at the backdoor and headed across the yard with some misgivings. The wooden door creaked open. He was greeted by powerful, yet familiar, smells. Stepping inside, he turned around and unbuckled his belt. Just as he was dropping his pants, he heard a faint sound coming from deep down in the hole. It was a small splashing noise that triggered an alarm in Eddie's mind. He reached around to check on his wallet, but it was gone. Turning around, he leaned over the hole, being very careful not to breathe. He squinted into the darkness, and as his eyes adjusted they grew wide in horror. There, at the bottom of the hole, sat his soggy billfold.

It was at this point Eddie's Ivy League education started to kick in. He refused to panic. Instead, he began to formulate a plan, listing his assets and liabilities. At the top of the asset list were his younger brothers. At the top of that list was his brother, Jimmy. Without any further ado, Eddie jogged back to the house and found his unsuspecting little brother.

"Jimmy," he said in a serious way, "I'm in trouble, and I think you're the only one who can help me."

"What's wrong?" asked Jimmy, innocently.

"Well, I've got a problem and I'm going to need someone brave to help me solve it. I'd ask one of the others, but they just don't have the courage it takes."

"You're right," Jimmy admitted, "I am pretty brave. What do you need?"

With that Eddie explained his predicament, and Jimmy agreed to help. But he would need to gather some equipment first. He ran upstairs and brought down a mask and snorkel. He went to the kitchen and grabbed a pair of yellow rubber gloves and some salad tongs. He stepped out to the shed and returned with a roll of tape and a length of garden hose. He taped the hose to his snorkel, slipped on the mask, inserted his hands into the rubber gloves and picked up the tongs.

"OOOHH HEY...EYE HEADY!" Jimmy said through the snorkel.

Eddie took that to mean, "O.K. I'm ready." He followed Jimmy to the outhouse, carrying the extra hose. Jimmy hesitated when he looked down. It was mighty dark, mighty deep, and mighty gross. But he WAS the bravest one in the family, and he'd given his word. He leaned over with the salad tongs and extended his arm, but he wasn't even close. He bent over from the waist, squirmed his shoulders through the hole, and stretched his arm as far as it would go. No luck. He still lacked about six inches. He came back up out of the hole.

"OOOOH GONNA HAAFA HOL ME."

Eddie understood that he was going to have to hold Jimmy. So, back down he went, and Eddie got a good grip around his legs. Jimmy's feet lifted off the floor as Eddie lowered him headfirst down the hole.

At that moment an evil idea came into Eddie's mind, an idea he regretted for the rest of his life. Even more, he regretted giving into the temptation. Just then, when little Jimmy was risking his life for his big brother, Eddie pretended he was letting go of Jimmy's legs. It was just the slightest little "Hoo-rah!", but it was cold-blooded and evil, just the sort of thing one might expect from a big brother.

In spite of the adrenaline rush, Jimmy managed to grab the wallet with his tongs and Eddie, weak with laughter, pulled him up out of the hole. Jimmy spun around and flung the billfold on the ground. He tore off the mask and snorkel and stared angrily into Eddie's bemused face. There were no words adequate for that moment, so after a couple of intense seconds he stomped away in disgust, muttering vague threats.

Eddie, on the other hand, was happy. He'd gotten his wallet back, he was home for the holidays, and Jimmy would probably forget the whole thing after a day or two. But that was where he was mistaken.

It was precisely after a day or two that nature called again, and Eddie found himself on a warmish afternoon enjoying an old National Geographic in the outhouse. As he flipped the pages, he was blissfully ignorant of the vengeance being planned by his little brother.

Again, Jimmy needed to gather some equipment. He checked through the kitchen cabinets until he found a can half-full of Red Devil Lighter Fluid. Then he rummaged through the drawers. His eye fell on a trusty box of Ohio Blue Tip Matches, the kind that you can strike anywhere. Armed and dangerous, he slipped out the back door of the house. He crept up the hill, by the graveyard and looked down on the peaceful outhouse. He snuck down to the old apple tree with the rope swing hanging from it and listened. He could hear Eddie humming a tune and he imagined him flipping through the pages of an article, perhaps "Spain, Sun-Drenched Splendor."

Without making a sound, Jimmy slipped up behind the outhouse where a loose board hung sideways. He popped the lid on the lighter fluid, and, aiming carefully, he began to squirt a stream through the crack. It puddled up around the left side of the seat. When there was a good-sized pool, Jimmy directed the stream to the right. Then, when all was ready, he squirted the stream back and forth to make a connecting channel between the two puddles. He set the can down and produced the Ohio Blue Tips. The match flared softly as he struck it, and without waiting, Jimmy flicked it through the gap in the boards.

"KAWHOOOOM!" Brilliant flames leapt six feet in the air around Eddie's ears. He screamed like a little girl and flung the magazine to the floor. He was convinced that this must be one of those fatal methane gas explosions you hear about in outhouses. He had to get out...fast. Leaping to his feet, he headed out the door, but he'd forgotten something. His britches were wrapped around his ankles! Helplessly, he felt himself falling. WHAM, he landed face-first in the mud. But he didn't have time to lick his wounds. There was an exploding outhouse behind him. Struggling to pull his pants up over his bare behind, he waddled toward the house, unaware of the barely stifled laughter coming from behind the outhouse.

Eddie learned a lesson that day every bit as good as his Ivy League education. In the words of the apostle, "Humble yourselves, therefore, under the mighty hand of God so that at the proper time he may exalt you." A good thing to keep in mind when tempted to get "uppity"!

Rat Man

As a scholarship boy, Eddie was given a job at the school. He was the "Rat Man." Eddie was thrilled to learn that he'd been selected to work in the Biology Department. Every day, he climbed the stairs to the attic of the Biology building and, pulling out a key he'd been given, he would open the door to the rat room. Exeter had an outstanding biology program that included advanced studies where experiments were performed on lab rats.

As Eddie entered the room, he was struck by the familiar smell of rat urine. It made him a bit nostalgic for the old outhouse. Around the walls, there were shelves of stainless steel cages with screen coverings. Eddie would walk slowly around the room, looking down into the cages. In each one, five or six rats would be waiting to greet him, stretching as far as they could on their hind feet and extending their pink paws toward the screen. There were cages with large, amiable males who reminded Eddie of friendly, slow-moving old dogs. There were collections of slim, nimble females, who were smarter than their male counterparts. There were cages with adolescent rats that rolled around and played with each other like kittens. And there were cages of new mothers with litters of tiny pink babies whose eyes hadn't opened yet. Eddie couldn't help but be reminded of his old friend, "Ratty."

When his feeding and cleaning chores were over, Eddie would sometimes take the lid off a cage and lift out a rat. He would sit on a table in the corner of the room and let it run across his shoulders and up and down his arms. Sometimes it would climb into his pocket or sit up on his lap to wash itself. When he was feeling homesick, it felt good to spend time with a little white friend.

But in the back of his mind, Eddie knew these rats were lab rats, and everybody knows what happens to lab rats. One Christmas, Eddie planned to break one of his little buddies out of jail. He was scheduled to fly home the next day, so he located a small cardboard box and put some lettuce and bread in it from the dining hall. After dark, he slipped into the biology building and climbed the stairs to the attic. Opening the door, he took out a flashlight and shone it into the cages. Dozens of little pink noses were raised to greet him. Thousands of whiskers twitched. What was Eddie to do? He couldn't take them all!

At last, he reached into a cage of adolescent rats and lifted out a small, silky female. He slipped her into his shirt pocket and turned to leave. Locking the door behind him, he hurried down the steps and back to his dormitory.

The next day, Eddie put the cardboard box into his backpack. When he got to the airport, he checked his suitcase, but carried his backpack with him. Every now and then, he'd open the top of the pack and peek inside. He inserted his hand and lifted the corner of the box, just to make sure his little friend was getting enough air. Then his flight was called.

Once Eddie was buckled into his seat, he carefully slid his backpack under the seat in front of him. The stewardess passed by to see that all was in order. She had no idea there was another tiny passenger on board. Eddie gripped the armrest as the plane took off, but eventually he settled down to look out the window at the sun glinting off frozen lakes and ponds below. He examined the motion sickness bag in the seat back in front of him. He took out the in-flight magazine and read it.

All of a sudden, he remembered his little friend! He put down the magazine and reached down to retrieve his backpack. When no one was watching, he opened it and peeked inside the cardboard box. To his horror, the rat was gone! He checked frantically through the socks and underwear in the bottom of the pack. Nothing!

Eddie began to panic, but nothing like the ladies in the aisle across from him would do if they felt a rat climb up their skirt! He unbuckled his seatbelt and squirmed around, trying to see under the seat ahead of him. Then he twisted to look behind him. Nothing!

At that moment, Eddie felt a faint movement in the seat beside him. Glancing down, he was flooded with relief. There, looking up inquisitively, was his little white friend. She sniffed the air and disappeared under his jacket. Eddie could feel her scrambling up his side. It tickled like crazy, but he couldn't risk laughing. He held his breath and bit his lip. Finally, the tickling stopped. He felt a warm little lump in his shirt pocket. Risking a peek, he saw his rat curled up, asleep. And she stayed asleep until the plane finally landed in Charleston.

Cat Hysterectomy

The next year, Eddie took one of those advanced biology classes. He worked on a month-long project on rats. First, he learned how to anesthetize them with a little cylinder of cardboard that had an ether-soaked cotton ball in it. Next, he learned how to operate on them. His experiment involved hormone related physiological changes.

What that meant was he had to neuter both a male and a female rat, and after a few weeks, put them down and do an autopsy to reveal what changes had occurred. It sounded pretty straightforward when the professor explained it to them, but when the moment came to kill his rats, Eddie struggled. He managed to go through with it, and even made a good grade, but he determined he'd rather operate on rats than kill them any day!

When he got home to West Virginia that summer, he was met by his brother, Jimmy.

"Eddie, I've got bad news," he said. "Dad says my cat, Tigger, is having too many kittens, and he's going to have to do something about it."

"Something about it" on a farm usually involved a gunnysack and the river.

Eddie looked up at the sky and stroked his chin. His mind was whirling. He thought about his biology experiment and his little brother's predicament. Rat...Cat...how different could they be?

"Jimmy," he said in his most reassuring way, "I can help you. I've been off to school, and I've learned a thing or two. Give me a few days to gather my equipment and we'll fix Tigger right up!"

A few days later, Eddie rode to town with his folks and made a stop at the drug store. Did they have a can of ether they would sell a sixteen-year-old? "Of course!

What else can we do for you?" Looking back on it, it makes you wonder.

When Eddie got home, he rounded up an old fish tank and an unused refrigerator rack. He found a piece of plywood that would work as a cover for the tank. Then, he made sure his mother's sewing kit was well supplied and asked to borrow the hair clippers. All was in place, so he waited until his folks were conveniently away one Saturday morning and assembled his brothers.

"Boys," he said. "We've got a problem. Dad is going to have to do something to Tigger if she keeps having so many kittens. But I've got a plan! Go get your bathrobes."

When the boys got back, Eddie had them put the robes on backwards, like surgeons, and cover their mouths with one of their dad's handkerchiefs. He spread a bed sheet over the dining room table and hoisted the old fish tank onto it. He poured a few splashes of ether inside, lowered the refrigerator rack onto wooden blocks and readied the plywood lid.

"Get Tigger," he said, and Greg and Gray raced off to produce the cat. She was lowered into the tank and Eddie capped the lid in place. Tigger looked a bit worried as she stared at the boys through the glass, but not for long. After a few seconds, she started to get sleepy and then lay down, unconscious. The boys pulled her limp form from the tank and spread her gently on the bed sheet.

"Jimmy," said Eddie, "this is your cat, so I'm giving you the most critical job. You're the anesthetist. You see this cone with the cotton ball in the end? It's got the ether on it. You have to carefully watch this cat and adjust the airflow. If Tigger starts to breathe fast, you pull the cone up closer over her face. If she starts to breathe slowly, you pull it back so she can get more oxygen. You got it?"

Jimmy nodded, deadly serious. He really loved his cat. He wasn't going to let anything happen to her.

Next, the hair clippers were produced and Tigger was carefully shaved down both sides of her body. The boys swabbed alcohol on the incision sites and then produced their mother's sewing scissors. Eddie made a three-inch incision down her right side and began to carefully probe, looking for her ovaries. He gently moved organs around until he located the uterus. Following it up, he came to the Fallopian tube which led to the right ovary. So far, so good! Taking a piece of white sewing thread, he carefully tied off the ovarian artery and then made a clip with the scissors. Lifting his head and smiling triumphantly he held the ovary aloft.

"That's one!" he said, "Now for the other! Jimmy, you O.K?"

Jimmy nodded, just a bit woozily from bending over the ether cone so intently.

The boys returned to the sewing kit and found a needle to stitch up Tigger's right side. Then they gently flipped the cat over and made the second incision. Again, Eddie poked and probed. He asked for more light. The clock ticked and time passed. After a half hour had gone by, Eddie was feeling light-headed as well. He'd looked everywhere and had not been able to locate Tigger's left ovary. Maybe his assumption that rats and cats were the same had been a bit optimistic.

After another fifteen minutes, Eddie made a tactical decision. Ovary or no ovary, it was time to close Tigger up. They stitched her left side together and removed the ether cone. The minutes dragged by as they waited for signs of life. Finally, Tigger blinked and let out a weak "meow." Eddie popped an aspirin in her mouth and rubbed her throat until she swallowed. Then, the boys put her in a box with a soft towel in the bottom and laid her in a dark corner to recover.

All was well...for three days. Then Jimmy came running to Eddie, his eyes open wide.

"Tigger!" he gasped. "She's chewed her stitches out! What are we gonna do?" he cried.

Eddie looked at the ground and felt like swearing. This hadn't happened in the lab. Well, there was only one thing to do. Fortunately, his parents happened to be away...

The bathrobes went back on. The handkerchiefs tied. The tank produced and ether splashed. Only this time there was something different. Tigger had the same worried look on her face, perhaps even more than the last time. Experience has a way of teaching even cats a thing or two. As she got drowsy, the boys saw she was having a strange reaction to the ether. It was producing thick mucus that drooled from her open mouth. Although she was slobbering profusely, Tigger still eventually dropped into a deep sleep.

Jimmy manned the anesthesia again and the boys went straight to the sewing basket for a needle and thread. There's a big difference between stitching a piece of cloth and suturing cat hide. The needle didn't want to go through. Eddie called for pliers and soldiered on. After a half hour, he finished sewing up one side and flipped Tigger over, avoiding the puddle of thick mucus around her head.

The second side proved even more difficult than the first. Minutes were ticking by, and everyone was growing tired. Just then, Jimmy looked down at Tigger and yelled.

"She's not breathing!"

Sure enough, Tigger was lying as still as death. Perhaps Jimmy had left the cone on too long. The boys started to panic.

"Don't worry!" he shouted, "I know what to do." Pulling an old toilet paper tube from his back pocket, he placed his home made "resuscitator" over Tigger's face and started to blow. She began to inflate like a fuzzy grey balloon. All the old movies used to say, "In with the good air, out with the bad." But the bad air didn't want to come out. Seconds were ticking by.

"Eddie!" yelled Jimmy, "Do something! She's going to have brain damage!"

So Eddie pressed down on Tigger's ribs. Nothing. He pressed harder. Still nothing! If he pressed much harder, he'd run the risk of popping the stitches he'd just worked so hard to put in. It was time for a desperate move. Eddie bent back over the still form of Tigger and put his mouth on the end of the toilet paper tube. He took a deep breath and then sucked back on the resuscitator with all his might. At that moment, the wad of mucus that had been blocking Tigger's airway broke loose. It traveled the length of the tube and struck Eddie square in the back of the throat. He staggered backward, crushing the toilet paper tube in his fist, and collapsed in the corner of the dining room. He struggled for air. When he could speak, he looked up at the circle of staring faces.

"That cat will die before I do that again!" he said with conviction. Jimmy went pale and turned to the limp form of his beloved cat lying helpless on the table.

"Tigger!" he cried. Then, without thinking of himself, he placed his mouth over the slobbery jaws of his cat and began to give her repeated puffs of air. Miraculously, she coughed and began to take wheezy breaths. She lived!

Looking down at the last remaining stitch, the boys made a quality decision; they decided that Tigger would just have to figure that one out for her self. They weren't going to put her back through the anesthesia again. They gave her the aspirin and tucked her into her box in the corner.

Two days later, Jimmy came panting up to Eddie again.

"She's done it again!" he said. "She's chewed her stitches out."

"Well, I'm done with her," said Eddie. If she makes it, fine. If she doesn't, she's no worse off than what was going to happen to her anyway."

Believe it or not, that cat healed up as if nothing ever happened to her. Who knows how many of her nine lives she used up in the ordeal, but Jimmy was thrilled to have her safe and sound... or almost. The following spring, Tigger gave birth to one little striped kitten. When the boys' dad found her and the kitten in the barn, he remembered his promise. But as he looked into the eyes of Tigger, he noticed a mysterious, tragic kind of expression. She looked as if she'd suffered great misery. Scratching his head, the boys' dad decided he could overlook one little kitten. Tigger would live.

Wings over Kitty Hawk

In some ways, Eddie's dad was still a kid at heart. Like the time he came out to go sledding with the boys when they were younger. A deep snow had fallen and the whole neighborhood had come out with sleds, toboggans, metal trays, and shovels to go sledding. They gathered at the top of a large bowl-shaped valley and, one after another, pushed off the edge. The kids would pick up speed as they raced down the hill, snow flying out behind them. By the time they got to the bottom of the long hill, they looked like dots.

Some of the bigger boys had constructed a ramp halfway down the hill, and the braver ones were risking their necks sailing over it, competing to see who could cover the greatest distance in the air. They'd put an old scarf in the snow to mark the record. When Eddie's dad showed up he surveyed the scene, his eyes lighting on the jump. As Eddie came panting up the hill with the small Flexible Flyer sled, his dad reached for it with a gleam in his eye.

"Dad," he asked with concern. "What are you going to do?"

"Why, I'm going to break the record over the jump!"

"Uhhh, Dad," Eddie hesitated, looking from the small sled to his dad's belly. "Are you sure? That's a pretty big jump…".

"Just watch," said his dad as he situated himself on the little sled and pushed off.

Eddie was about to get a practical lesson in elementary physics. Because his dad weighed more than the other kids, his sled picked up more speed. By the time he hit the jump Eddie calculated he must have been doing around sixty-five miles per hour. He sailed off the end of the ramp with a whoop and kept on sailing…ten, twenty, thirty feet it looked like. The scarf was far behind him when he landed. "Landed" may not have been exactly the right word. When the runners touched down, the weight of the impact drove them straight through the snow down to the dirt. The sled stopped dead in its tracks and the runners folded underneath with a screech. Eddie's dad lay spread eagle on the snow, not moving. By the time the boys ran down the hill, he'd managed to roll off what was left of the sled and was just recovering his breath. He picked snow out of his ears, nose and eyes and slowly rose to his feet.

He didn't have anything to say until that evening, when he took off his shirt. There, in every detail, was a bruise that perfectly matched the wooden deck of the sled.

"Does it hurt, Dad?" asked Eddie.

"A little," admitted his dad. "But we sure broke that record, didn't we?"

Eddie nodded. He wasn't going to say anything, but he was thinking the record wasn't the only thing that got broken.

While Eddie was at Exeter an article came out in National Geographic: "Happy Birthday Otto Lilienthal." It was about the first hang gliding championship that ever happened in the United States. It was a short article full of pictures of daredevils hanging under rickety bamboo frames covered with polyethylene sheets of black plastic. They were racing down hillsides until they gained enough speed to lift off the ground. They sailed along California cliff tops under brilliant blue skies. Their creed; "Fly no higher than you dare to fall."

As Eddie studied the photos, his heart began to race. He'd always wanted to fly! He thought of the ads for the Folboat and the resulting Mud Cat he'd constructed in the back room. Surely, a hang glider couldn't be any harder to build? So Eddie put fifteen dollars in an envelope and sent off for a set of instructions. When he got home from boarding school that summer, he was ready!

The first challenge was locating a source for long pieces of dry bamboo. In the end, a carpet store provided what was needed, as the carpets came rolled up on bamboo. He also picked up a couple of rolls of double-sided carpet tape. Then, he had to go to a building supply store for a big roll of .06mm. black polyethylene plastic. When everything was assembled, Eddie and the boys began to face the question of where to fly their creation. They'd learned a thing or two from their rat fishing experience about thorough planning.

The boys' dad came to the rescue by suggesting the family take its annual camping trip to the Kill Devil Hills of Kitty Hawk, where another pair of famous brothers invented heavier than air flight. The boys responded enthusiastically.

So it was that just a few weeks later the family set out in the old red and white V.W. microbus, complete with a hang glider lashed to the roof. They rolled down the West Virginia Turnpike, through tunnels into Virginia and down Fancy Gap Mountain to the North Carolina piedmont. Somewhere along the way, the engine blew up. Black clouds of smoke billowed from the back of the van and the boys were torn between the excitement of looking like the Bat Mobile, and anxiety over their delay in reaching the beach.

When they finally got to Kitty Hawk, they fought through clouds of mosquitoes to set up their tent. Woe be unto the one that left the door unzipped! Then they set about assembling their flying machine. The long bamboo poles were set out in a triangular shape, the famous "Delta Wing" designed by a man named Rogallo. They began to fashion a bamboo truss that supported the wing struts. A pair of shorter poles was attached to the truss from which the pilot would hang, swinging his legs and positioning his weight to control the glider. The bamboo pieces were lashed together and the black plastic unrolled. Using two-sided carpet tape, the boys rolled the black plastic onto the leading edges of the wing. When they stood back to admire their work, they resembled a small group of cavemen, gloating over the carcass of a pterodactyl they'd brought down.

Not far from their campsite, the boys spotted a likely looking dune. It was not too high and it was facing a stiff wind coming in off the sea. Together, they wrangled their contraption to the top of the hill and turned it to face the wind. While his brothers held the ends of the wings, Eddie jockeyed himself into the cockpit, hoisting the bamboo poles up under his armpits. On the count of three, they all began running down the dune, into the wind. Eddie heard the deafening flap of the plastic overhead and felt the bars lifting him off the ground. He remembered the hang gliders' motto; Don't fly higher than you care to fall. Fortunately, on his maiden voyage, he only made it three feet off the ground, a height with which he felt completely comfortable. The bird sailed for about twenty feet before it touched down and the boys were ecstatic!

Scotty took his turn, then Jimmy. Greg and Gray were allowed a go, but their big brothers held the ends of the wings. They were having a wonderful time. Then their dad walked over. He had a gleam in his eye and an excited smile on his face.

"Hey, boys," he said, "Can I have a go?" What could the boys say? After all, he'd been the one to bring them all the way to the beach just to fly the thing.

"Sure, Dad, but be careful..." Eddie said. He couldn't help but think of the Flexible Flyer.

"I've got this," said his dad confidently and hoisted the glider off the ground. Slowly he began to pick up speed. The boys ran alongside, stabilizing the wings. As their dad lifted off the ground, they released the wings and the glider began to gain altitude. But something was wrong. The nose lifted into the air and a puff of wind caught the glider under the right side. That wing rose high into the air, and the whole contraption began a slow death roll. In seconds, the nose was headed earthward and there was a sickening crash. The boys raced to where their father was extracting himself from the wreckage.

"Don't worry about me, boys," he yelled over the gusty wind. "I'm fine!" As the boys stared down at the crumpled frame and splintered bamboo of their glider, they didn't have the heart to tell their dad it wasn't really him they were worried about...

New England Champion

When Eddie was little, he used to be terrified of water. His momma would stick his feet in a tub, and he wailed like a banshee!

As he grew, his attitude changed. In seventh grade he decided he wanted to become a marine biologist and wished for scuba tanks and a neoprene suit so he could explore the green depths of the Coal River.

When Eddie got to Exeter, he struggled in the classroom but found his escape on the long, silvery reaches of the Squamscott River. As freshmen, the boys were placed in a sports program each term where they were exposed to the different sports offered by the school. When spring rolled around, it was time to try crew. The boys were marched down to the cedar shingled boathouse and loaded onto the "Barge." This was a wide, grey, flat-bottomed boat with two rows of seats and a walkway up the middle. The novice oarsmen would squat down onto their sliding seats, fit a long oar into the oarlock, and flail about as the barge pulled away from the dock. It was not a pretty sight, but Eddie was inspired and decided that when he returned to school in the fall, he was going to sign up for crew.

In the fall the coach looked Eddie over, all 120 pounds of him, and decided that he'd make a good coxswain. In addition to not weighing much, Eddie seemed accustomed to bossing boys around. The fact that he did it with such colorful language in a fascinating hillbilly accent sealed the deal.

Eddie got his start in the "club fours." These were four man "shells" that had a spot at the back where Eddie sat and steered. Each boat cost several thousand dollars, and he felt a great deal of responsibility to get it into and out of the boathouse without smashing it. His four underclassmen crew weren't quite as concerned.

To take the boat out of the boathouse was a precise, complicated maneuver. Eddie moved to the racks and stood at the bow of the overturned boat while his crew positioned themselves underneath.

"Hands on," he'd yell.

"Up on three. One, two three!"

"Off the rack on three. One, two, three!"

"Out of the house on three. One, two, three!"

The boys walked carefully through the large bay doors and down the ramp to the floating dock, Eddie walking behind to make sure they didn't accidentally hit anything. When they reached the end of the dock, Eddie would yell again.

"Over on three. One, two, three, over!"

"Down on three. One, two, three!"

The delicate shell splashed softly in the water. Then, taking turns, the boys would step carefully into the shell while their partners held it steady. They inserted their oars into the oarlocks, put their feet into the shoes, and laced them up. With a little help from one of the managers, they were pushed out past the end of the dock where they balanced the boat with their oars and made final adjustments. When all was ready, Eddie shouted again...

"Ready!"

"Ready all!"

"Row!"

And off they'd go, following the rhythm of the stroke oarsman who sat directly in front of Eddie. On the back of the shell was a small rudder connected by ropes to two blocks of wood Eddie gripped ferociously. When he pulled on the block of wood, the rudders would swing against the passing water, kicking the tail of the shell in the opposite direction. The shell would slowly respond and take off on a new heading. Besides steering, Eddie's other job was strategy. In a race, he would set the speed of the stroke and let the crew know how they were faring against the competition. He would encourage his crew by telling them when they were gaining, often calling out a "Power Ten", ten extra hard strokes to gain the length of a seat or two on the opposing boat.

Their home course was a beautiful stretch of tidewater bounded by marsh grass and farther off, low pine-covered hills. White seagulls wheeled overhead as the shell sliced through the dark, algae colored water. A sea breeze would riffle the surface of the river, bringing with it the organic smell of the estuary downstream. Out on the river, Eddie could forget about Latin verbs and geometric proofs. He was at peace...until race day.

Over time, Eddie moved up from the club fours to the racing eights. He began by coxing the number four, J.V, boat. Soon he was in the third, and then the second boat. By his senior year he was the number one Varsity coxswain. That year, Exeter had a really outstanding crew. They beat nearly everyone they raced. As December rolled around, and the season wound down, they were invited to the New England Championships on the Charles River. The course ran through the heart of Boston. Harvard, Princeton, and Yale had crews in the race. Along with other prep school crews, Eddie's boys were going up against the university freshmen. When the starting gun went off, Eddie leaned toward his crew and, with his neck veins bulging, screamed out the racing start cadence.

"Half, three-quarters, half, three-quarters, three-quarters, full, full!"

The long oars bent and the boat surged forward. Four boats were to their left and two to their right as they headed up the basin of the Charles. Eddie pointed the nose of his boat toward the center arch of the first bridge and called for a power ten. His oarsmen were swinging in perfect unison, their backs straining, their biceps burning. Icy spray flew off the whitecaps kicked up by the wind. As Eddie glanced to his right, he could see a boat falling behind. To his left the Harvard Frosh were in a dead heat with the Andover boat, Exeter's chief rival. Eddie looked his stroke oarsman in the eye and nodded.

"Up two on the next!" he yelled and thumped the wooden blocks loudly against the side of the boat. "Up two!" The pace picked up as they sailed out from under the shadow of the bridge and into a gradual left turn. Eddie looked looked right and saw nothing but the bank racing past. On his left, the Harvard boat had edged ahead of Andover, but was dead even with his boat. Eddie sighted down the river. The one mile mark was coming up. The river narrowed a bit and the chop was less. Time to make a move!

"Power ten on the next!" he hollered. "Drive ten!" He could hear his crew gasping for air. They passed under a second bridge, and when they emerged, they had gained a seat on the Harvard crew. Eddie looked ahead and saw the stands of screaming fans at the end of the straightaway. Glancing to the side, he saw his boat had gained another seat.

"Come on, boys!" he yelled. "We've got 'em by three seats. Gimme another!" He looked into the wild eyes of his stroke oarsman. Foam flecked the corners of his mouth. His sides heaved. He was in the race of his life! Still, the oars flashed in perfect synchronization, the boat leaping forward at the bite of each stroke. With a hundred yards left, Eddie's boys were a half-length ahead of the competition.

"Up two on the next!" Eddie called. Pounding the sides of the boat twice, he shouted again, "Up two!" putting the icing on the cake.

As the bow of their boat crossed the finish line, the judges blew a shrill blast on an air horn. Eddie gave the command to stop rowing.

"Ready all...way 'nuff!" His valiant crew collapsed on their oars. They were too exhausted to yell. Some leaned back to look blankly at the sky, others stared at the bottom of the boat, one leaned over the side and vomited. Slowly they began to recover, looking across the water at the other crews crossing the finish line, relishing the cheers from the stands. Smiles broke across their faces. They'd done it. They were the New England Champions!

When they finally made their way back to the boathouse, a tradition awaited Eddie. He maneuvered his boat through the icy slush until his guys could grab the dock. They held the boat steady as, one by one, they stepped out onto the wooden boards. Eddie was the last one out, and there were eight big guys standing between him and the safety of the boathouse. With a gleam in their eyes and a whoop, they pounced on him. Lifting him over their heads they paraded to the end of the dock. In an effort to match Eddie's hillbilly accent, the stroke oarsman yelled.

"Into the rivah on three! One, two, three!"

Eddie sailed high and far out over the frigid water.

He wished winning coxes didn't get thrown into the water at the end of the race, but this one time...he didn't mind it so much.

Over Bacon Falls

Between Eddie's junior and senior year at Exeter he went to a church camp for the first time. It was called Bluestone Conference Center. Run by the Presbyterians, it was miles out in the middle of nowhere, on a hillside overlooking Bluestone lake. Eddie had signed up for a five-day whitewater canoe trip. He was really looking forward to it!

Loading his things in the old V.W. microbus, his dad headed south through the town of Beckley and on to Hinton, WV, located at the confluence of the Greenbriar and New Rivers. Above Hinton, an enormous dam spanned the New River Valley, creating Bluestone Lake. Climbing up several switchbacks, Eddie and his dad rose from the valley and followed a country road running the ridges above the river. At last, they came to a weather-beaten sign that said "Bluestone Conference Center." It had an arrow pointing to a narrow lane leading precipitously over the hill. Another sign warned of overheating brakes. And with good reason. The "road" was more like a bobsled run, and by the time Eddie and his dad were reaching the bottom they could smell the peculiar stench of overheated brakes.

Just as they thought they'd have to stop to cool the brakes, they came around a corner and gratefully pulled into the camp parking lot. They entered the lodge, admiring its old wooden beams and large stone fireplace. Looking out from the front porch, their eyes swept the grassy knoll, taking in twelve to fifteen gray clapboard cabins. At the lower end of the hill was a swimming pool.

After registering, Eddie said goodbye to his dad and joined his group. A pastor was the adult leader and two college girls were to be the camp counselors on the trip. There were half a dozen teenage campers from around the state. After getting to know each other, they walked up hill to the old barn where the aluminum canoes and equipment were stored. The group began to sort through paddles and lifejackets, bailing buckets and tarps. They were each handed a waterproof bag into which they were to repack their clothes. Dehydrated meals were counted out and cooking equipment selected.

After a basic canoeing session down at the pool, the group headed out of camp to the wilderness area to spend the night. They walked on a winding lane through the summer woods. Sunlight filtered through oak leaves. Sassafras bushes grew in the shade. Alongside the road, velvety leaves of mullein mixed with bright splashes of Black-eyed Susans.

A half-mile around the mountainside, they reached their destination, the Hogans. Across the creek and up a steep bank from the bathhouse were two tidy wooden structures, each one with six beds. Smoky tarps were rolled up at the windows. The girls stayed in one, the boys in the other. In between was an established fire pit with a tarp stretched above. Before fixing their supper, the group had to lash together a picnic table from logs and boards. It was a standard team-building exercise.

In the morning, they climbed aboard the camp van, and with the canoe trailer rattling behind, they made the steep climb up the flank of the mountain. For an hour they wound through West Virginia, past mountain farms and upstream alongside the Greenbriar River, passing Alderson and Lewisburg. When the reached the small settlement of Renick, they turned off the highway and dropped back down to the river's edge.

The Greenbriar River is one of the scenic treasures of Wild, Wonderful West Virginia. It springs from the balsam covered highlands of Pocahontas County, and runs in class I and II rapids through three counties until it empties into the New River at Hinton. It's crystal clear waters are inhabited by rainbow trout and smallmouth bass. Below the town of Alderson, in a bend made famous by John Henry, roared the class III rapids of Bacon Falls. The story goes that the railroad company wished to avoid the long bend in the river by punching a tunnel through the ridge. It was there that John Henry challenged the steam drill and burst his heart in the effort.

Class I rapids are pleasant punctuation marks between still stretches of water. The current picks up, bubbling over rocks and carries the canoe along without having to paddle. There is little danger of tipping over if you're alert and avoid the rocks that form long inverted "V's" in the current.

Class II rapids can flip a canoe, if you're not careful. There is a larger volume of water and they require more technical skill to maneuver the boat from side to side as you navigate the rapids. Water rushing over shelves of rock can create "hydraulics", horizontal whirlpools that can trap a canoe and suck it back under the falling water.

Bacon Falls was a class III rapid, the biggest water that can be run in an open boat. After a couple miles of still water, the canoeist rounds a bend and faces hundred foot cliffs on the right. The river gathers momentum and drops into a long left hand turn. It roars over and around rocks and the paddler is thrown against the cliff. At the bottom of the run, waits a large bolder. Water piles up and around it to flip a canoe and leave its occupants dog paddling for the shore in the long pool below.

The group set off in high spirits, getting the feel of their boats and coordinating with their partners. They passed from shade to sunlight. The water sparkled and a refreshing breeze lifted the leaves on the trees. They were pleasantly tired when they reached their campsite a few hours later. Pulling the canoes up onto the sandy bank, they reached for tarps and cooking gear. In a bit, they were seated around a camp fire, opening dehydrated meals with curiosity. One powder turned into "Beef Stroganoff", another was supposed to be "Peach Cobbler." It took a bit of imagination, but all were famished and the food disappeared. In each packet was a flat slab of something called a "Bolton Biscuit." It may have been a modern version of sailors' "hard tack." During the trip, the campers enjoyed dropping pieces of their biscuits in the river to watch them expand to several times their original size.

The next morning was greeted with moans and groans. Blisters had risen, backs ached. Sliding their feet into cold, sandy river sneakers was torture. The pastor cheerfully encouraged everyone, saying they'd be sleeping on a bed that night. The group set out.

As the day progressed, spirits rose. The soreness was worked out of tired shoulders and the thrill of navigating rapids to see what was around the next bend kept everyone occupied. They stopped for lunch on a small island in the middle of the river and swam for an hour. As the sun dropped behind a ridge, the leader signaled a stop ahead. The canoes pulled onto the pebbly wash of a dry creek.

"And the beds?" asked the campers, looking around doubtfully.

"You're standing in it," grinned the pastor. "A creek bed!"

That night, everyone took turns stretching out on their sleeping bags to receive a back rub and a shoulder massage. Eddie's partner, one of the girl counselors, asked him to rub her shoulders. He'd never been too close to a girl before and wasn't sure how to give a massage, but didn't want to let his partner down. She started to make happy little sounds. He was amazed! He rubbed in circles, pressed harder, tried little karate chops, and she kept making happy sounds. When he finished she called her co-counselor over.

"Hey, you gotta try this! Eddie gives wonderful back rubs!" He gingerly placed his hands on her shoulders and began to move them in circles. It was like magic! She started to make the same sounds. Wow! He didn't know who was having more fun, his counselor or himself.

The next day the group pushed off again and headed downstream. They came to a part of the river where the current divided into several smaller streams separated by wooded islands. At the head of each island, large ramparts of dead trees and driftwood had washed up during floods. It made him wonder what this peaceful river might look like in high water. The canoes split up, each one exploring a different channel. Eddie and his partner threaded through a tight entrance and entered a long green waterway with ancient sycamore trees rising like pillars in a cathedral along both sides. Up ahead, they saw one of the trees leaning out over the water. As they got closer, Eddie could see the trunk was covered by large brown bumps. One of the bumps moved! There were about twenty unsuspecting mud turtles, sunning themselves on the log. Eddie wanted to get closer...his partner didn't! But Eddie was in the back of the canoe, and guess who steers? Eddie! He maneuvered the boat closer and the turtles began to get alarmed. He slid the bow under the trunk, and the turtles panicked. They began to bail out, landing in chunky splashes all around the canoe. One or two banged off the gunnels and Eddie's partner erupted in a screaming fit. Eddie was laughing so hard he could barely back paddle. For the next couple of miles, Eddie's partner refused to speak to him.

The next day was marked by long stretches of slow water. Large fish could be seen swimming slowly across a sandy bottom. After lunch, the pastor made sure everyone secured their belongings and checked the knots on their lashing. Before nightfall, they would be hitting Bacon Falls.

As the afternoon wore on, the tension began to rise. Around each bend, the campers expected to see the rocky palisades that marked the falls. Finally, a little before sunset, they heard an ominous roar coming from downstream. They paddled around one last bend, saw the cliffs, and noticed that the river seemed to disappear.

Their leader signaled a halt on the rocky shore above the falls and got out to reconnoiter. The campers followed. They watched the water slide glassily into the upper stretch of the rapids and turn to foam. The current pushed waves up against the base of the cliff. Water broke over the boulder that guarded the exit. Below the rapids, standing waves died out in a pool of still water.

"O.K. This is it." said the pastor. "The deep water is on the right side, against the cliff. Try to fend off of the rocks as much as you can. If anything goes wrong and you flip, keep away from your canoe and float down with your feet in front of you. Good luck with the boulder!"

And they were off. The first boat entered the rapids and began to pick up speed. They bounced down a couple of ledges and slid against the cliff. The campers fended off with their paddles and managed to keep going. At the bottom, they ruddered left as hard as they could and just missed the boulder. They lifted their paddles in victory in the still water below.

The second canoe followed. Halfway down, the bow struck the rock cliff and the stern swung into the current. The campers had no time to correct, and the canoe swept past the boulder backwards. Upright and in tact, the campers gave a whoop.

Eddie and his partner entered the current. He skillfully managed to avoid the rocks and ledges. Approaching the cliff, he angled himself away and paddled hard.

Success. Almost home free, he angled for the left side of the boulder; his partner angled for the right. The canoe struck the boulder broadside. Its downstream side was lifted on the pillowing water and the upstream side of the canoe began to take on water. Eddie threw a leg over the side and pushed off with all his might, but it was too late, the canoe had filled to the gunnels. With a supreme effort, they managed to pry the boat off the rock. Eddie and his partner, with water up to their armpits, paddled through the standing waves at the bottom of the rapid. They ignominiously accepted the rescue rope thrown to them, and dragged themselves to the sandy bank.

That evening they camped within the sound of Bacon Falls. Eddie's wet things hung near the fire to dry. While the others were setting up a campsite, Eddie hiked upstream to revisit the site of his demise. The river was full of rocks, and on a whim, he turned one over. To his surprise there were several large crawdads hiding underneath. He turned over another and found several more. It seemed all the crawdads from the still water upstream had congregated in this one place!

Eddie ran back to the campsite, forgetting all about his wetting and grabbed a bailing bucket. With a couple of friends he returned to the falls and in no time had a bucket full of large crawdads. They returned triumphantly to the camp and set a pot of water on to boil.

That night they enjoyed a hillbilly delicacy, boiled craw-dads. The only thing better was the nightly back rub!

When the week ended and it was time to go home, Eddie shook hands with his fellow campers. He looked around for his counselors, but they were in a staff meeting. Disappointed, he started walking toward the parking lot. Before he reached the car, the two girls came running out of the lodge. He turned around in surprise. First one then the other planted a big kiss on him. Wow! It was another new experience. Eddie realized kissing was even better than back rubs! He decided then and there he was definitely coming back to Bluestone!

Chapter Five
College, 1974-76, Age: 18-20

Eddie Dies

Eddie had lived away from home for three and a half years. When the chance came to graduate early, he leapt at it. He'd received an outstanding education at Exeter, but he'd learned things he wasn't so proud of. He managed to stay away from drugs, but he leaned to swear so profusely a friend made a recording. He collected Playboy magazines. He wasn't required to go to church, so he didn't. If you asked him about God, he'd just shrug his shoulders and say he didn't know.

Eddie had been so anxious to get home, he forgot what it would really be like when he got there. Scotty was still at Exeter. Jimmy had joined him. Greg and Gray went to school every day. Each morning, when Eddie woke up thinking of plans, he was disappointed to find his gang missing. He'd been away for so long he didn't really have any friends left in town. He began to get lonely (and bored, though he wouldn't use the word around his mother for fear she'd put him to work!)

One day Big Shelby, one of his father's co-workers, came by the house. Big Shelby was a big woman, closer to 500 pounds than 400. She'd had a hard life and carried a lot of bitterness inside her. She smoked, drank, and wasn't too particular about the company she kept. She was a fixture in the bars up and down the Big Coal River.

On this morning, though, Big Shelby came through the door with a smile on her face that lit up the room. She wasn't angry. She wasn't cussing. She was happy. The change was so radical and unexpected Eddie took one look and blurted out...

"Big Shelby, what happened?"

She laughed for one of the first times he could remember.

"I got saved!"

"What?" Eddie asked incredulously. He'd heard of people getting "saved" but never in a million years would he have guessed it would happen to Big Shelby.

"Yep, some friends invited me to their little church up the holler and I went. I ain't been the same since."

"I can tell," said Eddie, wondering if Big Shelby might have become a "Jesus Freak".

"Hey," said Big Shelby looking at him with a twinkle in her eye. "There's a service tonight. You wanna go?"

Although warning lights and alarms were going off in Eddie's head, he had reached the point of being just bored enough to try anything, even church up the holler.

"O.K." he said hesitantly.

"Great! I'll come around at 5:30 to pick you up." It was a done deal.

Sure enough, at 5:30 Big Shelby arrived in her beat-up car, and Eddie hopped in. They headed around the hillside, across the steel bridge, and up the highway, rounding curve after curve and passing one coal camp after another. They ran through places with names like Bloomingrose, Comfort, Seth, and Sylvester. When they reached Whitesville, they took a left and followed Clear Fork creek several miles deeper into the mountains. After forty-five minutes they reached the tiny settlement of Dorothy, West Virginia, "Unincorporated". Instead of turning up Booger Holler road, they crossed the creek on a wooden bridge and pulled up in front of a small white clapboard edifice with a hand-lettered sign on the front proudly proclaiming, "Dorothy Church of God of Prophecy". Eddie looked at the humble building and the beat-up, old cars parked out front. He fought to control a snigger. Wouldn't his prep school friends get a laugh out of this?

As Eddie walked up the concrete steps, he was greeted by a muscular coal miner, his wife and baby. Flashing a smile, the miner reached out a calloused hand and said,

"Praise God!"

Eddie was confused. When he'd gone to church in the past, people reached out their hand to offer you a bulletin. They didn't tell you what to do! But the man didn't seem angry; just the opposite. He was pumping Eddie's hand vigorously and just kept smiling.

When Eddie entered the church he followed Big Shelby up an aisle between battered pews. Along one wall sat a modified oil drum with a stovepipe rising through the ceiling above it. It glowed red in places from the burning coal inside.

As Big Shelby worked her way into a row, Eddie looked up at the platform. There he saw an elderly woman banging away at an old upright piano. To her left was a teen-ager working intently on getting his guitar chords right. Beside him was a kid flailing away at the drums with more enthusiasm that skill. Eddie thought to himself, "Drums? In a church? Is that heresy?"

As the service got underway, the forty or so simply dressed people in the congregation stood to their feet and began to clap their hands as they sang gospel hymns. Eddie had never been to a church where people clapped, but he timidly put his hands together and kept rhythm. The congregation made up for quality by the volume of its "joyful noise." They sang songs Eddie did not recognize.

"Jesus is coming soon, morning or night or noon.
Many will meet their doom; trumpets will sound.
All of the dead will rise, righteous meet in the sky,
Going where no one dies, Heavenward bound!"

After singing, the congregation entered a time of prayer...out loud...all together... with great fervor. Someone in the back was shouting. The coal miner to Eddie's right had tears running down his cheeks. A woman in the pew ahead began to speak in tongues and wave her hand jerkily. Eddie didn't know what to think. He'd never seen anything like it in his life. He'd heard stories about churches where the folks handled snakes, and he was halfway expecting someone to pull a wooden crate from under the front pew. He glanced around nervously for the emergency exit!

At last an old gentleman climbed the platform and approached the pulpit. He gripped it with gnarled hands and leaned across to stare at the congregation with a prophet's gleam in his eye. With an exhortation to "Praise the Lord", he launched into his message. Eddie squirmed. He felt like the pastor was speaking directly to him. He'd heard other preachers who talked as if they knew things about God. This elderly saint spoke as if he ate breakfast with the Almighty each morning. It was another new experience.

As the sermon concluded, the people sang another rousing hymn, buttoned up their old coats and stood at the door shaking hands and hugging necks. In spite of Eddie's shoulder-length hair, they hugged him too and warmly invited him to come back, soon! On the long trip home, Eddie was thinking that he'd just had the strangest

experience of his life...the drums, the singing, the shouting, the preaching. His wealthy, high-society classmates
would have thought it amusing and quaint. He tried that
attitude on, but it just wouldn't fit. Being honest with
himself, he had to admit he'd run into something he'd
never experienced before. Something powerful. In spite
of their poverty, the folks at that little church seemed to
have something his rich friends didn't.

Big Shelby invited Eddie to come back, and to his astonishment, he accepted. The third visit would prove to
be life changing.

Eddie had grown accustomed to the hugs and "Praise
the Lord's". He'd clap along with the music. It was the
preaching that hit him the hardest. As "Brother Tommy"
leaned across that pulpit, it was as if he were looking
right into Eddie's soul. Each word found its mark. As
Brother Tommy was concluding his message that
evening, he paused, and looking up he said,

"If they's anyone here tonight that wants to get right
with God, come on. Walk up here an' let us pray for you."

Eddie's heart was beating desperately. His heart
needed to "get right" with God. He knew what he had to
do, and slowly he rose from his place beside Big Shelby
and stepped into the aisle. He was met at the altar by two
white-haired grannies who laid their soft hands on his
back as he knelt before the Lord. He began to sob
raggedly, confessing sin and pouring out his heart. He

could feel the great Surgeon peeling away layers of his past life. He felt naked before his Maker. All his life, Eddie had struggled for love and acceptance. At each new school he'd wanted to be part of the gang; he craved to be on the "inside." He'd worked to learn funny stories, to play the guitar, to be a "nice" guy. But deep inside, he was still lonely and insecure. Then God spoke to him;

"It's time for the old Eddie to die. Open your heart. Allow my Son to come in and live his life through you. You must be born again."

With tears coursing down his cheeks, Eddie nodded his head and said, "Yes," to God. In that instant, his sins were forgiven. He was given eternal life. He was a new creation. The Heavenly Father says in his word that he gives a new name to his adopted children. Little Eddie, who'd grown to become just plain Eddie was now "Ed." It wasn't until years later that he found his name in the Bible. It is a Hebrew word that means "testimony" or "witness". For the rest of his life, Ed wanted to be a witness to the life-changing love and power of God.

Ed stood to his feet, smiling and sucking in an occasional ragged breath. He hugged the grannies. He hugged the pastor. He turned to the congregation and with a smile shouted, "Praise the Lord!"

When he got home later that evening, he walked in the back door and found his mother waiting up for him. With one look, she knew what had happened. She wrapped him in another hug. Still torn between laughter and tears, Ed said,

"Mom, for the first time in my life, I know what REAL love is!"

His mom could have taken offense. After all, she'd been the one that birthed him, changed his diapers, and cleaned up after him. But she'd had the same experience when she was a teenager, and she understood. She just hugged him closer and, patting his back, whispered in his ear,

"It's all right, honey. It's all right."

And it was.

"Go Big Ed!"

Ed had been thinking about what he was going to be when he grew up and where he wanted to study. He wasn't one hundred percent sure, but he thought he might make a good teacher. One thing he WAS sure of; after four years of living far away, he wanted to go to school close to home. As it turned out, there was a college, a teachers' college, just on the other side of Charleston. It was within hitchhiking distance. It was affordable. There was only one small hitch...It was for African Americans.

Ed considered lying about his race to get in. In the end, he learned that West Virginia State College had recently integrated and now allowed white students to study there. The vast majority of them were day students, but Ed planned to live on campus. He was invited to spend a weekend at West Virginia State during the summer to get acquainted with the school.

Ed was assigned a roommate for the orientation weekend. His "roomie" was named Roger. Roger was an interesting specimen. He stood just under five feet tall...on tiptoes. He made up for his short stature with long blond hair that cascaded down his back to a spot below his belt. It might not have reached so far on a taller man.

Roger was a typical teenager, never having lived away from home. He was ready to sow some wild oats. Ed, on the other hand, after his years at boarding school, was practically a cosmopolitan. In the evening, after a presentation from the ROTC group on campus, Ed returned to his room in the eight-story high rise dorm and got ready for bed. No sign of Roger, or his hair!

At around two-thirty in the morning, Ed heard someone fumbling at the door. It opened, and someone shuffled in, knocking over a lamp in the process. Ed sat up in bed and reached for the light switch. He saw a pathetic sight. There, slumped over a desk, was a frazzled blond hairball, holding his hands to his face and moaning.

"My eye....Oooohhh, My eye, man!"

"What happened?" asked Ed.

"Man...me an' some dudes were smoking pot. I was

gettin' pretty high. When I went to light another joint, I missed the joint and stuck the match right in my eye, man!"

"Hmmph..." Ed snorted and turned over to go back to sleep. Kids these days!

Ironically, Roger joined the ROTC in the fall and shaved every bit of his blond hair off. Had he not been only five feet tall, Ed might never have recognized him.

When it came time to report to classes in the fall, Ed was assigned to the seventh floor of the same high-rise dormitory. The hall was populated largely by members of the football team...and Ed. There were nearly four thousand African-American students living on campus...and Ed. Oh, there may have been five or six other white students, but who was counting? It was a very peaceful campus with hardly any racial tension; if a fight broke out between the races, it wouldn't last more than a second. Eddie made friends quickly and became a mascot for the football players who lived on his floor. He was reassured when they told him,

"Ed, if any of the 'brothers' go to messin' with you, just let us know. We'll take care of it!"

That was good. What he wasn't sure about was what to do when those same football players started "messin'" with him. One day as he was walking back from the shower room, a towel tied around his waist, they grabbed him. Laughing mischievously, they dragged him to the elevator, and held him until the door opened. They pushed Ed inside, hit the button for the lobby, and jerked his towel off. Then they headed down the hall to Ed's room, congratulating themselves on their prank.

Ed had to think fast. The lobby was always full of dozens of students, guys and girls. He spun around and hit the button for the next floor. When the door opened, he raced down the hall to the fire exit. He crashed through the metal doors, dashed up the stairs, and pulled the fire door open. Before his friends realized what happened, Ed had beaten them to his door, stepped inside, and locked it! As they banged on the door, all they could hear was his satisfied laughter.

Ed was interested in extra-curricular activities. He joined the Baptist Student Union, though he didn't feel very Baptist. He played tennis with his roommate. One evening, he went out for a run on the college track. He decided to see how fast he could do one lap, a quarter mile. To his amazement, his watch showed 47 seconds, close to world record time! The next day Ed approached the coach who arranged to meet him at the track that afternoon. After nearly killing himself, Ed flopped down at the coach's feet.

"Not bad," he said. "But closer to 60 seconds than 47. Why don't you think about training with our cross-country guys?" Ed just thought about getting a different watch!

Ed took a course in children's theater. The professor was a Christian who loved drama but said he preferred to work with children because it was a healthier environment. Ed, who was expressive and had a big mouth, excelled and was given the lead role in a play called "John Willy and the Bee People." That was how he found himself stepping out of a space ship onto center stage of the Charleston Civic Center one afternoon.

He was excited to be given one of the leading roles in a production of "The Screwtape Letters." His character was the poor mortal who was being influenced by a bungling junior demon. It was a great role! Ed got to be in a fight scene. He got to be in a drunk scene. He even got to be in a kissing scene! There was just one little problem; aside from a quick kiss at camp, Ed had no experience. He had no idea how to kiss a girl, much less do it in front of an audience. The mere idea made him blush.

For the first few rehearsals, Ed and the girl would get to that scene and nervously say, "And this is where we kiss." Only they didn't. A week before the performance, the girl approached Ed and said,

"What about the kiss?"

"Um...yeah." replied Ed.

"You want to practice?"

"Um...well, I guess we should," said Ed in an unconvincing way.

The girl took his hand and led him behind the backdrop. She stepped closer, tilted her head back, and closed her eyes. Ed felt giddy, like he was about to faint. He gathered his nerve, held his breath, and leaned over. He bumped roughly into her face and almost missed her mouth.

"Uh..." said the girl. "Maybe you ought to try again."

"You sure?" he said.

"Trust me." she answered. She tilted her head back and closed her eyes again.

Ed took better aim and brushed his lips against hers. "There," he thought, "That wasn't so bad." The girl disagreed.

On the third go round, Ed landed one right on the kisser and held it for a few moments. He was beginning to like this! The girl thought they'd practiced enough.

When the night of the performance came, the hall was packed. Up in the back sat Ed's enormous roommate, Larry. He covered two entire seats. Larry was the center for the football team. When he came through the door to their room, he had to turn sideways. Ed had told Larry about the kissing scene, and Larry had turned out for moral support. The show began.

Apart from receiving a minor bruise, the fight scene went well. The drunk scene was worthy of an Academy

Award. As the kissing scene approached, Ed's mouth got dry and his pulse quickened. It was one thing to kiss this girl behind the backdrop; it was a totally different thing to do it in front of a live audience! But the show must go on.

At the thrilling climax to the play, the girl stepped close to Ed, tilted her head back, and closed her eyes. The moment of truth had come. Ed inhaled deeply and decided to go big or go home. He reached around the girl's waist, spun her around, and leaned her over backward, planting a world-class smooch on her lips. From the back of the auditorium there was an eruption. Ed's roommate, Larry, was standing on his seat, waving his arms in the air and shouting with all his might,

"Go Big Ed, Go! Go Big Ed, Go!"

The End of an Era

"Hey, Ed! Everybody's heading out to Charlie's farm this weekend. Wanna go?"

Ed did want to go, but he hung his head and mumbled, "I can't"

"Why not?"

"I have to go home. My mom is having a baby."

At nearly twenty years of age, it was a little embarrassing to say your mom was having another baby. She'd already had five. It had been nearly ten years since the last one. What were his parents thinking?

One thing his mother was thinking was that she was tired of not having running water in the house. Oh, she joked about her "running" water as her sons ran out the back door with buckets, racing up the two hundred yard path to the well and back. Wash days were murder. She made it a bit easier on her kids by doing three loads of laundry with just one machine full of water. She started with the whites, then the colored clothes. By the time she was washing the boys' jeans, the water was only a bit less muddy than the jeans!

Not having running water in the house was a hardship on everyone, but she was putting her foot down. She refused to bring a new baby home if there was no toilet and sink. After all, what was so great about an outhouse? It was cold in the winter, drew flies in the summer, and it was such a long way from the house! When it eventually filled up, a new hole had to be dug and the outhouse drug over to the new spot. One time, when the family had just moved the outhouse, their cow got in trouble. Unaware of the change, she walked across the fresh dirt sprinkled over the old outhouse hole. When the boys heard the cow bawling, they popped out the back door to find her sunk up to her chest. He bony hips and back end were still high in the air. It took a rope and a concerted effort to haul "Punkin" out of that hole, and nobody wanted to go near her for a long time after that.

The day finally came when their father lugged a shiny white porcelain toilet up the hill. He chivalrously gave up his little office in the back room and began sawing a hole through the floor to install pipes. Ed and his brothers had spent long hours digging a trench from the well to the house. Electric lines were hung and a pump was lowered to the bottom of the well. A hole for the septic tank was dug and a drain field put in. It was a monumental effort, and the boys hoped their baby brother would be worth it!

When at last the family gathered for the first flush, they were thrilled to watch the water magically disappear down the drain and hear a trickle refilling the tank. No more long trots across the back yard. No more accidents with chicken poop and bare feet. No more squatting on chamber pots at night. It was a great day. It reminded Ed of a joke he'd heard:

A little country boy was watching the plumbers install an indoor bathroom in his house. When he saw that it was fully functional, he raced out to the family outhouse, perched on the creek bank. He was going to fulfill a lifelong dream. He put his shoulder to the outhouse and heaved. It began to rock. He heaved some more, and it rocked harder. With one last shove, the outhouse fell over the bank and landed with a satisfying splash in the creek. The little boy happily watched it float away.

That night at supper, his father looked up from his plate and asked,

"Anybody know what happened to the outhouse this afternoon?"

The little boy's eyes got big, but he answered bravely,

"Yes, Papa. I cannot tell a lie. I shoved it in the creek."

His papa stood up, took hold of the scruff of his son's neck, and hauled him out back to the wood shed. After a good whipping, the little boy stood rubbing his backside.

"It ain't fair, Papa." he said. "We studied George Washington in school and when he told the truth about cuttin' down the cherry tree, his papa didn't give him a whippin'"

"Maybe so," admitted his papa, "But they was one big difference..."

"What's that?"

"His papa wasn't SITTIN' in the tree when George cut it down."

The Rattlesnake Belt

It was the spring of the year and Ed's dad had asked him and Scott to do some fencing in the upper pasture. This meant lugging a hundred-pound roll of barbed wire up the hill. Ed cut a sapling and stuck it through the hole in the center of the roll. Then, lifting the ends of the sapling, he and Scott headed up the trail, being careful to keep it level so the hundred pounds of barbs didn't accidentally slide off onto either one of them. Scott carried a hammer and "U" shaped nails called staples. Eddie tucked some wire pliers in his back pocket and carried the wire stretcher in his free hand. Some people have never used a wire stretcher. It is a medieval looking tool that consists of a long wooden handle tipped with metal teeth. Part way up the handle is a short chain with a metal grip on the end. To stretch the wire, you pull it as far as you can by hand and grab it with the metal grip. You set the teeth of the wire stretcher into the fence post and, using the long handle for leverage, you stretch the wire out until it vibrates. While you hold it taut, your partner drives a staple around it into the black locust post. Most fences take four strands of wire.

Ed and Scott had been back and forth over the same spot three times already, lugging the unwieldy roll of wire up over rocks and through the underbrush. They were on the last strand. Just as they were stepping across a downed tree, Scott heard a sound. It was one of those sounds you don't want to hear in the woods, a sort of buzzing sound. Some would call it a "rattling" noise.

They dropped the roll of wire and leapt backwards. There, coiled perfectly under the bottom strand of wire, sat an enormous timber rattlesnake. It's triangular head was raised over the glistening diamonds on its back. The tail, sporting a long chain of bony rattles, was raised in the air and was vibrating rapidly. Ed turned pale as he looked at Scott. They both realized that the rattler hadn't just appeared. It'd been sitting there all along as they'd hauled the wire up and down the hill. At any moment, it could have chosen to bite them, but it hadn't!

As the first shock wore off, they stepped closer to examine the snake. It was huge and it had recently shed its skin. The sunlight struck its scales, giving them an iridescent sheen. It really was a beautiful creature. Ed thought it would make an amazing belt. Gathering his nerve, he picked up the wire stretchers and approached the snake. With great care, he placed the metal teeth on the snake's head and pressed down with all his weight. He did it again. The snake continued to thrash around, even though it was dead. Ed had seen that before and wasn't worried. But he and Scott still had a half-hour of work to do before heading down the mountain, and he didn't want anything to happen to his snake. He built an enclosure with rocks and dropped the rattlesnake into it. He capped it with a large flat stone. Then he and Scott went back to work.

As they finished up and were heading back down the mountain, Ed stopped off to pick up the snake. Without thinking much about it, he lifted the flat stone and immediately leapt backwards. There lay the rattlesnake, coiled and ready to strike!

"These snakes are one hard thing to kill!" he thought to himself. So he killed it again. For good measure, he pulled the wire pliers out of his back pocket and pulled the fangs out of the snake's mouth. Even if it came to life again, it wasn't going to bite him.

When the boys got home, Ed skinned the snake and tacked it's hide to a long board, being careful to stretch it and put salt on it. Scott took the meat inside and fried some up for the boys. Coming from the mountains, they liked to brag that they ate snakes.

After a few days, the skin was dry. Ed took it off the board and began to scrape it with his pocketknife. He'd found an old, cloth Boy Scout belt. When the snakeskin was ready, he wrapped it around the belt and ran it through his mom's sewing machine. To finish it off, he took some black paint and a small brush, adding two reptilian eyes to the burnished brass of the buckle. It was a masterpiece!

That summer, a van-load of affluent teenagers passed through on a tour of Appalachian poverty. They'd heard of the work Ed's father was doing and wanted to meet him. One afternoon they climbed the hill to the old farmhouse. They sat in the shade, drinking well water out of mason jars, listening to stories of the work in the War on Poverty. Ed and his brothers were amused by these city kids. The visitors pitched a couple of tents in the back yard and prepared to spend the night. One of the guys raced to the house, breathlessly announcing that two of our chickens were fighting! When Ed went out to check, he saw an old rooster mating with a hen. He snorted and said,

"Son, those chickens aren't fighting. They're doing just the opposite."

One of the girls was a real beauty. Her name was Allyson. Ed looked for chances to sit close to her and talk. When the time came for the group to leave the next day, Ed asked for her address.

Over the next couple of months, Ed wrote to Allyson often. Allyson...not so much. When Ed leaned that a friend of his was driving north, he arranged to join him. They spent two days on the road before ending up in the high-class suburbs of New York City. Allyson's father was an important attorney. They lived in a large home under spreading elm trees. Ed realized pretty quickly that he was in over his head.

After a couple of days, it was time for Ed to head back to "Snake Eatin' West Virgina." He left his rattlesnake belt and a piece of his heart with Allyson. She handed him a blue shirt with pearl buttons. On the long road home, Ed pondered his adventure and came to a conclusion. Allyson had gotten the better end of the deal!

The Sleeping Porch

Ed was always looking for ways to toughen up his younger brothers, whether they needed it or not. One strategy had been to camp out on the upstairs porch all summer. In the fall, before heading off to college for the first week, he suggested to Greg and Gray that they continue sleeping on the porch until Christmas. He said it would make men out of them. In many ways, Greg and Gray were already twice the men Ed was, but they took the challenge...on one condition; every weekend, when Ed came home from college, he had to sleep out on the porch with them. By November, Ed was regretting his challenge.

One Friday afternoon, early in December, Ed set out from Institute, West Virginia, hitchhiking his way home. He had to catch rides along the Kanawha River up through Dunbar and South Charleston, over the bridge and past the state capitol. Then he'd work his way to Marmet, where he'd leave the Kanawha valley and ride up Short Creek and over the mountain to Racine. Saying goodbye to his lift, he'd still have to hike a mile around the hillside to get to the farmhouse on the hill. Normally, the forty-minute drive would take an hour and a half to hitch hike.

This December evening everyone seemed to be in a hurry to get home. The clouds were turning a dark grey and settling down to snow. A last pale ray of sunlight flickered through the clouds as the early darkness closed in for good. Ed stood on the side of the highway, his backpack on and his thumb out. He'd gotten as far as the turn off in Marmet, but no one seemed to be heading up Short Creek holler; at least no one willing to pick up a hitch hiker. It began to snow, fat flakes drifting down through the darkness and piling up around his boots. Ed stepped into the Seven Eleven store once or twice to warm up and check on the time. It was getting late.

At a little after ten, a big Crown Victoria sedan pulled off the road. Ed was so grateful for the ride, he didn't notice the official insignia painted on the doors. He pulled the handle and jumped in, just grateful to be out of the cold and wet. When he looked over at the driver, his heart skipped a beat. There was one of the biggest policemen Ed had ever seen. He immediately wondered if he'd done something wrong. Was hitchhiking still legal? Was this man going to take him to jail?

Ed was relieved when the man offered his hand and began to speak.

"Sheriff Johnny Protan," he said. "At your service. It's a cold one, ain't it?"

Ed nodded, a little tongue tied.

"Where you headed?" asked the sheriff.

"I've been away at college. I'm headed home for the weekend," said Ed.

"Where do you live?" asked the sheriff.

"Around the hill from Racine, halfway to Bloomingrose."

When the cruiser pulled up at the intersection in Racine, Sheriff Johnny Protan signaled to cross the bridge.

"Oh," said Ed, "You can let me off here. I'm used to walking."

The sheriff looked over at him with a fatherly grin and kept driving. He threaded his way through the town and around the windy road, his windshield wipers knocking the snowflakes away. At the bottom of Ed's hill, the sheriff let him out of the car. Ed walked around to the driver's side, shook his hand and thanked him.

When Ed reached the house, he stepped inside and knocked on his parents' door to let them know he was home. They'd waited up and were glad he was O.K. He grabbed a sandwich and a glass of milk, then headed up the narrow stairs to bed. Slipping out of his jeans and shirt, he remembered his promise and pulled open the door to the upstairs sleeping porch. He was met by a blast of cold air.

Greg and Gray were fast asleep under every sleeping bag the family owned. ON top of the sleeping bags was a light dusting of snow, but the boys were toasty warm under all those blankets. Toasty warm sounded good to Ed. Instead of going off to look for some more covers and climbing into a freezing cold bed, he had a brainstorm. Why not just ease in between his two warm little brothers? He gently turned Greg onto his left side and Gray onto his right. As quietly as he could, he eased himself into the deliciously warm crack they left behind. Pulling the covers over his head, he said a simple prayer of thanks and started drifting off to sleep.

"Hrmph," muttered Greg as he turned back to the warmth. He brought his knees up and they connected sharply with Ed's thigh. Greg had some of the boniest knees in the family!

"Wmrgh," said Gray and rolled to his left. His elbow caught Ed squarely in the adam's apple.

"Hrmph," said Greg again in his sleep and pulled the other knee up.

"Wmrgh," mumbled Gray and nearly blinded Ed with the other elbow.

Ed spent a long time that night thinking about how warm he was. He surely didn't sleep much. Mostly he regretted having challenged his brothers to sleep out until Christmas. As far as he was concerned, Christmas couldn't come soon enough!

Home Economics

Jimmy was finishing up his junior year at Exeter and he decided he'd had enough. He'd skipped other grades in the past, why not skip his senior year of high school and go straight on to college? He began to research the possibilities.

Ed was doing well at West Virginia State College, so he was a bit surprised when Jimmy called to suggest a change.

"Come on, Ed," he said, "It'll be fun. We could go to the same college and be "B.M.O.C's."

"What's a B.M.O.C." asked Ed, not sure he wanted to be one.

"Big Men On Campus," answered Jimmy. "With my looks, brains, and charm and your...uh, your...personality, why, we could take any college by storm! The girls would be lining up to go out with us."

Ed wasn't so sure, but Jimmy kept insisting. At the end of the conversation, Ed promised to think about it.

The next week Jimmy called back.

"I've got it," he said with complete sincerity.

"What?" asked Ed.

"The college we're going to attend. Longwood College in Virginia."

"Ummm, I've never heard of it." stalled Ed. "Why would we want to go there?"

"It's a Home Economics college!" said Jimmy. "It'll be great!"

Sometimes Ed wondered about his little brother. This was one of those times.

"What would we want with a degree in home economics?" asked Ed.

Sometimes Jimmy wondered about his big brother. This was one of those times.

"Who cares?" replied Jimmy. "The thing is, there are 1,500 girls at the college and only three guys."

Ed and Jimmy didn't go to Longwood College, but they did wind up going to college together the next year at Saint Andrew's Presbyterian College in Laurinburg, NC. It was a small school with only about 500 students where their Uncle Bill was a math professor. Because it was such a small school, they were sure it wouldn't be too hard to become B.M.O.C.'s.

Chapter Six
Becoming a Man,
1976-1978, Age: 20-22

Saint Andrews Social Club

Ed and Jim arrived at St. Andrews in the fall, ready to be Big Men On Campus. It was a lovely place, the drives lined with pink dogwood trees. There was a large lake in the center with residential halls on one side and academic buildings on the other. Every day, students would cross a causeway to class, enjoying the view of old cypress trees lifting their knobby "knees" around the edges of the lake. The dining hall was on the edge of the water and students marked the birthdays of their friends by dragging them out of the dining hall and tossing them into the lake.

It was a bit of shock for Ed. He was coming from a very secular, ungodly college where the band, Earth, Wind, and Fire, was about as spiritual as things got. He'd seen students doing drugs and girls slipping into boys rooms after hours, but that was to be expected. He assumed things would be different at a "Presbyterian" college. They weren't. If anything, they were worse! Preachers' kids, who'd chafed at having to be good all their lives, would buy a keg of beer as soon as they got to college and drink it dry as fast as possible. Classes were of minor importance. It was interesting to note that many of those freshmen didn't come back after Christmas; the ones who did paid more attention to their studies.

Ed and Jim began to make friends with the students who weren't drunk. They'd hang out with their buddies, laughing and telling jokes or going to the gym for a swim or bowling. They made friends with the "good" girls that lived on one hall in the women's dorm, often stopping by to visit and hang out. One day, Ed discovered two hairs growing on his chest. He felt so manly and proud, he had to show someone, so he walked to the girls' dorm. He bumped into his friend, Carol, and said,

"Hey, Carol, Look at this!" He pulled down the neck of his shirt.

"What?" asked Carol. "I don't see anything"

"There. Right there," Ed insisted. "I've got two chest hairs!"

"Wow, " said Carol sarcastically. She lowered her collar. "I've got five!"

Ed, Jim, and their friends wanted to come up with a name for their group. They settled on the S.A.S.C. This was code for The Saint Andrew's Stud Club, because they were pretty sure they were the best looking guys on campus. To tone it down a bit for general consumption, they publicly called themselves The Saint Andrew's Social Club, which may have been a lot more accurate.

Ed, Jim, and their friends had hit St. Andrews just as the disco era was exploding. They bought Saturday Night Fever shirts and platform shoes. They leaned how to do the Hustle, the Funky Chicken, and the Bump. One of their favorite dances was the Washing Machine. It was a dance they made up. They'd pretend to put a quarter in the washer, add a little detergent and bleach, and begin to agitate. With shoulders gyrating, they'd move around the floor until it was time for the spin cycle. Then, it was everybody for himself! Ed was feeling more comfortable around girls and not quite so shy. They liked to dance with him, so he learned more dance steps. Little did he know that one day he'd be showing middle school kids how to disco dance at his first teaching job!

Ed and Jim also ran track and cross-country. Jim, though he was younger, was faster, but both made the varsity teams, competing in five-mile cross-country races and the half-mile and mile races in track. They'd take off for long training runs through the sand hills of Eastern North Carolina then come back to campus where Coach Blackie Blackwell would have them run a few "pyramids" until they felt like throwing up. It did make them faster though!

At his last race of the season, Ed was entered in the mile run. He lined up with his brother, Jim, another boy from their school, and several runners from other colleges. The gun went off and away they went. Ed was feeling good that day...very good! He led the pack around the first turn and headed down the straightaway. After the first lap he was still in the lead. After the second lap no one had passed him. He was running faster than he'd ever run. The third lap in a mile race is a killer. The lungs start to burn; the legs start to go. As Ed headed into the bell lap, a runner from another school passed him, then another. With his lungs on fire, he pushed himself as hard as he could go; he would never run another race at St. Andrews. When he finally crossed the line, he was back in third place, but looking down at his watch, he broke out in a huge grin. "4:53." Not only was it his personal best, it tied the fastest mile his dad had ever run. He was very satisfied.

After the race, Ed and Jim grabbed their gear and hopped into the back of a conversion van with several of their friends. They were headed across the state to spend the weekend with a friend, Christy, in her hometown of Spartanburg, South Carolina. They dropped their things off at her house and went out that evening to cruise around town. As they approached the main intersection in downtown "Sparkle City", Ed suggested they do a Chinese Fire Drill. When they came to the stoplight, everyone was to jump out of the van, run all the way around it, and jump back in before the light changed. Everyone on the sidewalk and waiting at the light would be left staring. It was just something silly college kids did for fun.

Eddie decided to make it a bit more interesting. He was still in his skimpy track outfit, though he'd put on some sweats over top. This was at the height of the "streaking" craze, so he decided he'd pretend to go streaking. When the van stopped at the busiest intersection in the city, Ed and his friends all tumbled out the back and started to dash in a circle around it. They were yelling and screaming; everyone stopped what they were doing to watch. As he pulled around the back fender, Ed ripped off his sweatshirt. Going past the driver's window, he pulled off his running shoes. All his friends were in front of him, so they didn't understand why the people were staring and mothers were covering their children's eyes. As Ed passed the passenger window, he slipped out of his racing shirt, leaving only his sweat pants. He knew full well that he had on his racing shorts underneath, but the people didn't know that. As he came around the last corner, his friends were tumbling into the open doors of the van. He stuck his thumbs into the waistband of the sweat pants and jerked them to the ground. Then, laughing, he jumped into the back of the van and closed the door. The van pulled away, but Ed could still hear people laughing. When he looked around, his friends were pointing at him and laughing so hard they could barely breathe. Looking down, Ed realized he'd made a mistake.

Instead of only sticking his thumbs into the waistband of his sweat pants, he'd stuck them all the way into the band of his racing shorts. He was sprawled on the floor of the van in the altogether! His face turned red, and he desperately reached for his sweats. That was the last time he ever went "streaking."

Trinidad and Tobago

Ever since God changed Ed's heart, he wanted to tell other people about it. He wanted his life to be a witness to God's mighty power and great love. He felt like he had a mission to the mixed-up kids at his college. They desperately needed what he'd found!

Ed joined the College Christian Council at St. Andrews, and in a short time he was given the responsibility of lining up speakers for weekly chapel talks. Every week, thirty or forty students would gather in the student center to hear a local pastor talk about the Christian life. One week, the invited pastor canceled, and Ed wasn't sure what to do. He felt like God was saying, "You talk to them."

Ed was a little nervous about getting up in front a big group of his fellow students. He tried calling some back-up speakers, but no one was available. As he went to bed the night before the chapel talk, he turned off the large Japanese lantern he had hanging over his bed. He rolled on his side and said to his roommate, Chip,

"What do you think I ought to do?"

Chip was a country boy from Kentucky. He answered in a slow drawl,

"Why don't you pray about it?"

That sounded like a good idea, so in the darkness Ed began to pour his heart out to God. Should he speak? Shouldn't he?" Would the Lord give him some kind of sign? No sooner had the words come out of his mouth than the Japanese lantern over his head flared on. One, two, three seconds, and then it abruptly went off. It had never done it before, and Ed's hair rose on the back of his head. He suddenly felt as if he were in the very presence of the Almighty. Chris brought him back down to earth when he drawled from the darkness,

"Didja see that?" he asked. "I reckon you oughtta speak."

Ed's mother met some Spirit-filled Presbyterian ministers in Charleston. They were going to preach at a crusade in Trinidad and Tobago. She'd always wanted to go on a mission trip, but Baby Billy needed her at home. So she signed Ed up for the trip!

It just so happened that students at St. Andrews spent their January doing educational travel or taking an intensive, month-long course. When Ed approached his advisor with the idea of a missions trip, he thought it a wonderful idea. So it was that Ed found himself lifting off from snowy Yeager Field in the dead of winter, headed for the Caribbean.

Missions was something Ed had never really considered. He loved adventure, and he'd lived a very cross-cultural life, but he just didn't feel called to be a missionary. When he and the three pastors landed in Port of Spain, Trinidad, he was stunned by the tropical sun, the brilliant colors, the East Indian accents. They drove through the bustling city where music groups were tuning their steel drums in preparation for Carnival. They passed out into the sugar cane fields and rolling hills of the countryside. Pastel colored houses lined the dusty roadside. Ed was enthralled. They drove through the largest town in the northeastern part of the island, Sangre Grande, which Ed could translate as "Big Blood." He'd heard stories of voodoo in this part of the world and the thought of Big Blood was a bit unsettling.

At last they pulled through the gates of the orphanage where they'd be staying for three weeks. It had a sign across the top that read, "Heart's Home", printed across a large red heart. Inside the compound, nearly twenty-five children were sitting, studying, and playing around the courtyard and under the shade of a large mango tree. Three or four colorful buildings made up the compound; a dormitory for the boys and one for the girls, a kitchen/dining room, and staff house. Behind the dwellings were several long chicken pens that provided a small income for the orphanage. Above and behind that was a forested hill with tangerine trees dotting it.

The pastors left for visits or services each day while Ed stayed behind to help around the orphanage. He liked playing with the kids, swinging them around in circles until he felt his arms would pop out of their sockets. He helped in the kitchen, one day butchering a dozen chickens for supper. He pitched in with the chicken pens, filling sack after sack with manure to get the pen ready for the next batch of pullets.

In the evening, he would sit and visit with the pastors or with the young American couple that ran the orphanage. They had some wild stories to tell about hearing voodoo drums in the woods behind their house, of red fireballs that floated across the compound at night and occasionally attached themselves to people's sides, of clawing noises on the outside of their bedroom doors. Ed paid close attention when they explained their way of praying for God's protection. They called it "spiritual warfare," and it involved taking their rightful authority as God's children over the schemes of the Devil. Ed began to pray more earnestly before going to bed each night.

One morning, as Ed was coming back from a training run, he was met at the entrance to the compound by one of the pastors.

"Ed, in my devotional time this morning I think I received a word from God for you."

Ed had never had a word from God; he felt a little nervous, but he nodded his head and the pastor continued.

"I feel like God wanted me to tell you that you will never have money problems."

Ed was relieved. He hadn't known what to expect, but this sounded pretty good! Of course, the years would teach him that this didn't mean he would have a lot of money. Many people who have money worry and fret over it. It just meant that he would not have problems with money. Great!

As the three weeks drew to a close, Ed realized he'd come to love his new little friends. He'd put a lot of time into making them laugh. But he was ready to head home. In his journal that last evening he wrote:

"I've had an amazing time these past three weeks. Met a lot of incredible people and heard some wild stories. I came here wondering if perhaps God wanted me to be a missionary. I've prayed about it sincerely, but thankfully, I haven't felt a call to missions. What a relief!"

Thirty-five years later, Ed found this same journal. He was sitting on a hillside in southern Mexico, up to his ears in missions work. He had a good belly laugh.

Student Teaching

Ed worked hard in his classes and made good grades. He was pretty sure he'd enjoy being a teacher. During the spring semester of his last year, he was assigned to a middle school out in the country for his student teaching experience; his subject was Eighth Grade Science.

Ed had always been a bit of a "ham," and he enjoyed performing for his students. They really liked it when he did experiments that included setting things on fire. He soaked a dollar bill in alcohol and put a match to it. Since alcohol burns at such a low temperature, the dollar bill didn't catch on fire. He showed them metal could burn by lighting a strip of magnesium on fire. It flared up with a brilliant white light. The students were awed at first and amused later because Ed accidentally set his grade book on fire. They also enjoyed the days Ed would bring his guitar to class. It didn't have much to do with science, but it had to do with the students and they loved listening to "Country Roads" and "I'm Leavin' on a Jet Plane."

For his final project, he created a unit called "Spaceship Earth" that compared the planet to a spaceship and explored the ways food, water, air, and waste would have to be recycled and managed for a long voyage. His supervising teacher was impressed and the kids seemed to learn a lot.

When Ed's last day of student teaching came around, the school threw a party in the gym. They had him sing,

"I'm Leavin' on a Jet Plane." Some of the girls cried. As they filed out of the gym, the boys and girls shook his hand. All at once, one of the more daring girls reached up and kissed him. Then they all wanted to. It was so embarrassing!

Before graduation, Ed's advisor approached him with a big smile. He reached out his hand to congratulate Ed. Then he pulled a plaque from behind his back. On it were written the words "Student Teacher of the Year."

Copperhead Cabin

Ed returned to Bluestone Camp, this time as a counselor. He thought he'd died and gone to heaven! He felt like he'd been born to work at camp. He knew the woods, he knew how to lead a bunch of kids on adventures, he played the guitar, he loved to share from his Bible around the campfire.

The kids liked having Ed as their counselor. He took them "creek stompin'" and caught crawdads to boil and eat. He showed them what a sassafras bush looked like and taught them to make sassafras tea. They climbed trees and made mud slides. They built "homes in the woods", complete with Lazy Boy recliners made of rocks. They tried to make history at Bluestone, doing things no one had ever done before. They called themselves the "Lucky Dogs" because they got to be in his cabin.

One memorable night, as his group was gathered around the campfire for devotions, he was interrupted by anxious whispers coming from the far side of the circle. A couple of the kids were looking off into the dark woods behind them.

"What's wrong?" asked Ed.

"Do you hear something?" they replied. It was the wrong question to ask a bunch of city kids out in the woods on a dark night. Given half a minute and just a little imagination, those kids could hear just about anything, whether it was real or not. Ed had to respond decisively.

"Don't worry," he said bravely. "I've got this. But I'm going to need a flashlight." In seconds a heap of flashlights appeared at his feet. Choosing the two strongest beams, Ed set out through the darkness in the direction of the noise. His campers cowered close to the fire, wondering what they'd do if their counselor was killed and the creature came for them.

Ed picked his way across the ravine and around a couple of fallen trees. Sure enough, there was something out there. It was moving towards him, making enough noise to wake the dead. Leaves rustled, branches snapped. Images of large carnivores began to take shape in Ed's mind. Just as he decided it would be smart to get out of there, he spotted motion in the beam of his flashlights. Ed froze. It moved closer, making even more noise! Was it a bear? A mountain lion?

Just then two black, beady eyes caught the light. A small nose twitched in its beam. The black and white coat revealed a baby skunk, out for a midnight stroll in the woods. Ed released the breath he'd been holding, and started to laugh. Who would have thought such a tiny creature could make such a racket!

But there were things that Ed didn't like. Most of his fellow counselors were not "born again" believers. They were more like the freshmen Ed had known at St. Andrews; nice enough people, but tired of "religion" and lacking a passionate relationship with God. On the weekends, between camps, they would hang out in the craft lodge and drink beer. Ed was troubled for two reasons; as a teacher, he recognized that time at camp was an incredible teachable moment, and he wondered what kids in the other groups were learning. On the other hand, having only recently learned what true love was, he passionately wanted to share it with his campers.

So it was that he found himself, a week before his second summer at camp, heavy-hearted and concerned. He made a bold decision. Before returning to camp, he was going up into the hills, like Jesus, to fast and pray. He wanted to be prepared spiritually for this important ministry. He was not responsible for the other counselors, but like Pastor Tommy of the little Pentecostal church where he'd been saved, Ed wanted more than to just know something "about" God; he wanted to hear from Him directly, to stand barefoot before a burning bush.

Ed collected his Bible and a notebook. He rolled up his sleeping bag and filled a couple of milk jugs with water. He put on his boots, grabbed some matches, and let his folks know where he'd be. Then he headed out the door. As he passed the spring where the ponies got watered, he heard a noise behind him. There trotted their yellow, beagle-mix dog, Glory. Her tongue lolled out the side of her doggy smile and she looked up at Ed hopefully.

"Go home!" said Ed and turned to head up the hillside.

Five minutes later, he heard something behind him trotting through the leaf litter. There was old Glory, still hopeful, still smiling.

"Go home, I said," warned Ed. He picked up a stick and threw it in her direction. She was unfazed.

"O.K," conceded Ed. "But don't say I didn't warn you." He headed back up the steep hillside quietly pleased to have the company.

Ed and Glory reached the ridge line and turned north, following old fire roads into the backcountry. He was heading to a place he'd discovered while rambling through the mountains. It was an old hunters' cabin built of un-chinked logs. The hilltop site had been cleared of trees to make the cabin, and a thicket of thorny blackberry vines had grown up around it. The building was small, just big enough for a bunk bed of rough lumber and a spot to make a fire on the dirt floor in the corner. It had no door.

After hiking for three miles, Ed was glad to set his water jugs down and unroll his sleeping bag on the rough boards of the bunk. He took a long drink then pulled out his Bible. He set a goal for himself of reading through the entire New Testament before heading home. He would underline passages that might be useful in his work with campers and make notes in his notebook.

Pausing to take a drink from time to time, Ed worked his way through Matthew, Mark, Luke, and John. The stories came to life and fit together in meaningful new ways. The sun set and Ed lit a small fire in the corner of the cabin. His stomach rumbled, so he took a long drink of water. Then he stretched out to get some sleep. Old Glory hopped on the bunk and curled up comfortingly against his back.

The next day he read about the apostles, filled with power from on high, witnessing to what they'd heard and seen. He continued as Paul preached his way through Asia Minor and wrote inspiring letters to the young churches. His notebook filled, his water jugs emptied. Night fell again, and Ed built another small fire in the corner. He slipped off his boots and crawled into his sleeping bag, Glory in her spot close beside him.

Around two o'clock, Ed woke with a start. Glory was on her feet, barking furiously. Ed sat up and looked around. The cabin was pitch black, and Ed regretted not packing a flashlight. He made Glory quiet down and listened. Then he heard the sound of rustling leaves, not coming from outside the cabin, but from inside, just a couple of feet from where he lay! He'd grown up in the country, so he didn't panic. It could be a mouse or a squirrel; why, it might even be a baby skunk! He reached for a boot and tossed it in the direction of the sound. Whatever it was, froze.

Ed stopped to process this information. When a boot is thrown at a mammal, its instinct is to run away. Reptiles, on the other hand, will freeze. He picked up his other boot and tossed it. The thud was immediately followed by the uncomfortably familiar buzz of a rattlesnake. Even so, Ed didn't panic. Again, he processed this information. He'd heard too many stories of hikers who'd woken up with a rattlesnake in their sleeping bag. Being cold blooded, rattlesnakes seek out warm places, and Ed was certain he didn't want to be one of those warm places. He came to the conclusion that this cabin wasn't big enough for him and a rattlesnake.

Rolling up his sleeping bag, Ed scooted to the foot of the bed and calculated the distance to the door. He'd have to put his foot down one time; he prayed it wouldn't land on the snake. Gathering his courage, he leapt for the door and was outside the next second, safe and secure. As he peered into the darkness, he realized he was surrounded by over an acre of prickly blackberry vines. He might be "safe" but he began to wonder how "secure" he was. All of a sudden, he had a brainstorm. He could climb the corner of the log cabin like a ladder and reach the shed roof. It might not be the most comfortable spot to pass the night, but he was pretty sure he'd be free of snakes.

Once on the roof, Ed slid into his bag. Then his bag began to slide down the roof. He wriggled his way back to the ridgepole like an inch worm and tried to go to sleep. He tossed, he turned, he scooted back up to the ridgepole. After a half hour he sat up, feeling sorry for himself. He was alone, in the dark, on the backside of nowhere, sitting on a roof over a rattlesnake in the middle of a briar patch. Then God began to gently speak. He asked Ed why he'd come to this place. Wasn't it to spend time with Him? Could he get much closer than on top of a roof on top of a mountain? Humbled a bit, Ed agreed and began to pray.

He prayed for his campers. He prayed for the other counselors and for the director. He prayed for the churches that supported the camp. He prayed for his family and friends. He prayed until he was just about prayed out, but as he came to the end of his list, he found there were things hidden under it; deeper things that lay closer to his heart. He started to cry out to God about the secret fear he kept hidden. He wanted so desperately to find the perfect girl and get married, but as he was approaching the end of his college days, he was still as single as he'd ever been. He was certain he'd graduate and return to West Virginia to become a teacher. He could picture the only bachelorette in the county as being a hog farmer's daughter. Covered with badly-done tattoos, she spend her time hoisting Pabst Blue Ribbon beer in some bar perched on the river bank. It was a scary thought!

He prayed harder. As he did, the Lord drew close and in that intimate moment, He showed Ed a different picture; a pair of strong arms gently holding a tiny baby.

"Ed," said God. "Do you see that baby? That's you. You see those arms? They're mine. Don't worry. I've got you. As it says in my word, "My grace is sufficient for you." So, if you never get married, just trust me. My grace will be sufficient. And if you get married next week, you may need even more grace! But my grace will always be sufficient for you."

Ed felt a deep, supernatural peace flood his spirit. He relaxed, breathed a deep sigh, and fell asleep. Moments later a raindrop hit him right between the eyes! In denial, he scooted further down into his sleeping bag. Then he had to scoot back up to the ridgepole. More raindrops fell. Time passed. Scoot down...scoot up...check the rain.

At around 6:00, Ed sat up and looked around. Off in the east, the first pearly light of dawn was beginning to suggest itself. Ed tossed his sleeping bag off the roof and climbed down the damp logs. He peered into the gloomy cabin. There was light to see that no snake had climbed to the top bunk. Ed was just exhausted enough and still filled with enough peace to convince himself that he'd be okay to catch a couple more hours of sleep on that top bunk. After all, hadn't God promised that His grace would be sufficient?

At around 9:30, Ed opened his eyes to see sunlight filtering through the cracks in the cabin walls. It was time for business. He climbed down from the top bunk and made his way to the boots lying in the dried leaves on the floor. He picked up first one then the other and shook them out. Nothing. He stooped down to look under the bunk. Nothing. He turned to the far corner of the cabin where the fire had been. With the last piece of firewood, he poked at the ashes...

A triangular head on a long neck shot straight at him from the shadows. He leapt backwards, adrenaline rushing through his body. The serpent uncoiled from the dying warmth of the ashes and stretched itself a good five feet across the cabin floor. Ed kept his cool, waiting until the snake's head was just over a flat slab of rock. At that moment, he brought the stick of firewood down with all his might. The snake writhed, trying to escape the hail of blows, but Ed persevered. Five, six, seven times he struck the serpent, wanting to be sure it was truly dead. He'd had bad experiences in the past with snakes that were only "partly" dead.

When he was certain he was out of danger, he lifted the snake on his piece of firewood and carried it out into the sunlight. He was surprised to discover that it wasn't a rattlesnake. It was the largest copperhead he'd ever seen. Evidently, either kind of viper reacts to stress by shaking its tail. In the dry leaves, the copperhead had sounded like its cousin. He draped its enormous body across a bush growing beside the door.

Ed had drunk all his water and only a few pages of the New Testament were left to read before heading home. He was deep into John's revelation, engrossed in the account of an evil dragon intent on waging war with the offspring of a woman. When he came to the last "amen," he closed his Bible and gathered his few things. Stepping outside, he nearly had a heart attack. He'd forgotten about the copperhead! For a second, he thought he was back in Revelation. Then he remembered the last verse of the book and heaved a sigh of relief.

"The grace of our Lord Jesus Christ be with you all. Amen." Revelation 22:21

Debbie Kay Plyburn

One week later, Ed pulled into Bluestone camp, ready and rarin' to go. He dropped his gear on a bunk and greeted the new guy counselors that had come for orientation. Then he headed to the lodge to "help the girl counselors carry their things to their cabin." His motives may have been questionable, but he did end up making several trips, hauling suitcases and sleeping bags to the girl counselors' cabin. He also met a long-legged girl named Debbie Kay, whose folks were dropping her off for the summer.

Debbie had grown up coming to Bluestone as a camper. It was her favorite place in the world. As an eleven-year-old, she'd given her heart to Jesus at a camp-fire on the point overlooking Bluestone Lake. The counselors had played an old Simon and Garfunkel tune, "Bridge Over Troubled Waters". As the moon rose above the distant ridge line, Little Debbie's heart responded to the words:

When you're weary, feeling small
When tears are in your eyes, I'll dry them all
I'm on your side, oh, when times get rough
And friends just can't be found
Like a bridge over troubled water
I will lay me down...

Her counselor wasn't sure what to make of Debbie's tears, but her Savior understood and embraced her at that moment.

She came to camp every summer after that until she got too old to be a camper. This summer she was coming as a counselor for the first time. Although she didn't need any orientation, she threw herself into the week's activities; hiking, singing, and laughing heartily. She quickly made friends with all the counselors. She was thoughtful, sweet, and kind. To borrow one of her own phrases, "she had a heart as big as Texas." It was obvious she also had a personal relationship with Jesus. Her Bible was well used.

Bluestone camp operated on a small-group philosophy. A guy and a girl counselor would be "Mom" and "Dad" to a mixed group of eight or ten campers. They would build their "home in the woods" where the campers would cook out, play games and have vespers. As it turned out, Patty, the program director, assigned Ed and Debbie to work together in Hogan C for the first week. Ed was happy because he knew Debbie loved the Lord and because he thought the campers would love Debbie. They did.

Together, Ed and Debbie planned each day's activities. They cooked breakfast over the campfire. Then they boiled water to wash the dishes in. They carried buckets on their hikes to pick blackberries and turn them into campfire cobbler in the dutch oven. They walked to the camp pool where Ed performed his famous "Buzzard Dive" and amazed the kids by how far he could swim under water. They made sassafras tea. They boiled crawdads. They sang around the campfire and spoke quietly of God's love. When the week was over, tears ran down cheeks as good-byes were said. It had been the best week of Ed's life and he was going to miss working with Debbie.

To his surprise, Patty assigned Ed and Debbie to work together again the second week. Their friendship was growing deeper. They worked together like a hand and glove. It touched Ed to see how much Debbie loved the kids in their group, and how much they loved her. He had to admit, there was something very special about her.

Amazingly, Ed was assigned to work with Debbie for a third week in a row. It was now the hottest part of the summer and fatigue was setting in, but Debbie's cheerful attitude and kindness didn't wane. One afternoon, their group signed up for a cookout. They collected their crate of food and headed to their campsite. Blue-black clouds gathered in the west. Gusts of hot air lifted the leaves and kicked up little dust devils. It was getting ready to rain, and Ed secured the tarp over their camp fire. If you'd signed up to cook out, you cooked out; period.

The skies ruptured and a chilly cascade sent the campers dashing under the tarp. They were cold, tired and hungry; the outlook was bleak. Ed ran out into the rain and gathered an armload of wet wood. Back under the tarp, he began to break it into smaller pieces, hoping for some dry heartwood he could use to start the fire. Just as a tiny flame was flickering to life, the bulging tarp filled to the brim and a small stream of water spilled over the side. It fell harder, splashing into the center of the fragile campfire. The campers, T-shirts clinging coldly to their backs, began to complain. They weren't having any fun. Ed could feel the pressure mounting. He was doing all he could.

At that moment Ed detected movement at his side. Looking to his left he saw something that amazed him. There was Debbie, on her knees in the mud with a large camp spoon. She was digging a trench as hard as she could to channel the falling water away from Ed's fire. Her wet hair hung in scraggly strands along her cheeks. Her hands and knees were covered with mud. Ed thought he'd never seen a more beautiful sight! In that moment, his admiration turned to love.

He had no idea how Debbie felt. She was so sweet and kind to everyone, there was no way to tell if she had any special feelings for him. A couple of weekends later, the camp lifeguard invited all the counselors to her big, old, country house for the weekend. They pulled up to pillared porches, high-ceilinged parlors, and a country kitchen that was warm and inviting. After a big lunch, the group headed to the back of the property where an opening yawned in a limestone outcropping. One by one they entered the cave. Ed made sure he was close to Debbie, shining the beam of his flashlight so that she could see where to step, reaching out his hand to steady her as she climbed.

That evening the group decided to spread their sleeping bags out on the upstairs porch. Again, Ed made sure his sleeping bag was close to Debbie's. He had something important to tell her, if he could just get up the nerve! The others laughed and talked until they began to drift off to sleep. Ed kept talking softly to Debbie until he was sure no one else was awake. The waxing moon was peeking through the porch railings. His heart was beating like a drum when he finally found the courage to speak what was on his mind.

"Um, Debbie. I've really loved working with you this summer."

"Me too," said Debbie quietly.

"I suppose you'll be going back to a boyfriend after camp?" Ed forced himself to ask. His world hung in the balance of her answer.

"No," she said, "I don't have a boyfriend. Never have."

"Really?" Ed swallowed. "Really!" Fireworks were going off in his head. Daring to keep talking, he said, "Then is it O.K. if I tell you I'm crazy about you?"

Debbie was quiet for a moment that felt life forever. When she finally spoke, Ed's heart turned upside down.

"I'm pretty crazy about you too."

Ed doesn't remember sleeping for the rest of the night. He was in heaven. What was the name of that magical place? Union, West Virginia.

When Ed and Debbie got back to camp the next day, they got some interesting news. There weren't enough campers for the week to keep every counselor busy. They could either take the week off or they could join a small group of teenagers on a 100-mile whitewater canoe trip down the New River. They looked at each other and smiled.

Putting in the river at Radford, Virginia, the group was to make its way one hundred miles downstream, through several class two and three rapids, across the state line, and into the calm waters of the Bluestone Lake. They would take out at the bottom of Gas Line Hill and walk the trail up to the camp lodge.

That week was a hazy blur of happiness for Ed. Just as he and Debbie made great co-counselors, they also made great canoe partners. He fell in love with the sight of her long, sun-kissed back as she sat in the bow and pointed out rocks. They worked together effortlessly, maneuvering through the rolling whitewater and bubbling eddies. In the evening, they pulled their tired bodies ashore and relaxed in the firelight, listening to the music of the river as it flowed by. On the water they talked and talked, covering topics from Christmas traditions to future plans. Each bend opened a new vista of tree-covered slopes and rocky cliffs. Each mile opened new horizons in Ed's heart. By the time they paddled the last few miles of still water down Bluestone Lake and pulled up at the take out point, Ed was convinced Debbie was God's answer to his prayer and that one day he would make her his bride. God's grace had been sufficient!

Ed and Debbie dated long distance in the days before Facebook and texting. They wrote long mushy letters that passed from Ed's college in North Carolina to Debbie's in Kentucky and back. They made cassette tapes and traded them back and forth. Once, Ed learned that a friend was driving from St. Andrews to a business interview in Cincinnati, Ohio. He skipped class to ride along. It was a twenty-two hour round trip for an eighteen hour visit, but he was in love and nothing else mattered.

The next summer, they were back at Bluestone, but the director had the sense to put them in different groups. That didn't stop them from catching quick meetings during the week and going on long walks on the weekends. Their favorite rendezvous on a hot afternoon was the walk-in cooler behind the kitchen where they shared a Dreamsicle and a couple of cool minutes together.

They returned to college in the fall; Ed for his final year and Debbie for her next to last. At Thanksgiving, Ed traveled by bus to Barboursville, West Virginia, Debbie's hometown. She picked him up out on the highway in her old green Oldsmobile. When they pulled into the drive at 1402 Long Street, Ed got a surprise. Debbie's father, brother, two male cousins, uncle, great uncle and grandfather were lining the sidewalk from the driveway to the front porch. With the most serious expressions, they shook Ed's had firmly and searched his face for any hint of insanity or criminal inclinations. He reached the end of the gauntlet, his hand aching, but happy to have passed the test. They didn't know it, but he carried a diamond ring in his pocket!

Debbie's dad, Bill Plyburn, was to become the mayor of Barboursville in time. He was a man who knew his own mind. He'd made it clear that no young men had better come sniffing around his daughter until they met five conditions:

1. A good job
2. Money in the bank
3. A vehicle
4. A house
5. A diamond ring

Eddie started out without any of these items, but he was extremely motivated. By that Thanksgiving, he either had those items or he had a plan to get them. He was ready for "the talk". Debbie and her mother invented an urgent need for something from Bill's drug store and suggested Ed ride along. Sweating profusely, he climbed in the passenger seat, and after the car pulled onto Long Street, he began his memorized speech. Asking for the hand of Mr. Plyburn's daughter felt a lot more awkward than it had in practice. There was a long, nerve-wracking pause, and then Bill said,

"Well, Ed, I don't know you as well as I'd like. A girl's father wants to be very careful about who his daughter marries. There is one thing I do know. Whenever you're around Debbie is the happiest I ever see her. If you'll promise to take good care of her and keep making her happy, you have my permission to marry.

As Bill told the story afterward, he described Ed as kneeling in the floorboards, trembling. In spite of that, Ed had a good relationship with Bill who often called Ed his "favorite son-in-law." It didn't matter that Ed was his ONLY son-in-law!

Years before, Ed's father had given him and his brothers a piece of good advice about proposing marriage. He'd said,

"Boys, when the time comes to pop the question, whatever you do...don't take the girl to a romantic restaurant. With those flowers on the table and that violin music, ANY girl is going to say "Yes". No, that's not the way to be sure you have the right one. What I recommend is this; on the hottest day in August, load your girl-friend up with a fifty-pound backpack and take off hiking down the railroad tracks. Once you've walked about ten miles, and she's just about ready to drop, you pop the question. If she says "Yes", she's a keeper!

Ed had missed the August date, but before sitting down to Thanksgiving dinner, he invited Debbie to slip away with him for a few minutes. Walking hand in hand through the drizzle of a remarkably unromantic after-noon, they made their way to the railroad tracks. Stand-ing on the damp cross ties, Eddie shifted the umbrella to his left hand and reached into his pocket. Pulling out his grandmother's diamond ring, he opened the box and looked into Debbie's big, green eyes.

"I'm still crazy about you," he said. "I want to spend the rest of my life with you. Will you marry me?"

This time there was no pause. She wrapped her arms around him, and after a big kiss she said, "I'm crazy about you, too! Yes!"

Just the Beginning

Little Eddie had grown to become Eddie. Eddie grew to be Ed. He married Debbie Kay Plyburn on the 23rd of June, 1979, a day of afternoon storms and rainbows of promise. He was no longer a boy; he was now a married man. Ed and Debbie drove off in a red pick-up truck to a little home perched on top of Droop Mountain. They were both going to teach school in a hamlet called Hillsborough, West Virginia. They had no idea they would eventually have eight children, swim in the crystal waters of the Bahamas, fight badgers and 37 degree below zero temperatures in northern Wisconsin, lead a thousand children to Christ at South Mountain Christian Camp in North Carolina, or found a multi-ministry center called El Monte on a hillside in southern Mexico. But God did! And every step of the way, his words to Ed on the roof of that snake-infested cabin have proven true...

"My grace is sufficient for you." 2 Corinthians 12:9

About the Author

Ed Somerville is the firstborn of six rambunctious brothers. In 1968, his father, a Presbyterian minister, moved the family to the hills of Appalachia to help fight the War on Poverty. He chose to live like the people he ministered to. A falling down house without plumbing? No bathroom... no problem!

Little Eddie and his brothers could have cared less. They roamed the hills, skinny dipped in the river, rode ponies and ran wild. Well, half wild. Their mama was always there to haul back on the reins when needed.

From that hillside, Ed went on to attend the finest boarding school in the nation, then a historically black college. He married a brave girl named Debbie and they started a family that would grow to eight children. They bounced from a Christian school in the Bahamas to a sub-zero winter in northern Wisconsin before relocating to the Blue Ridge mountains of North Carolina. Ed baptized over 1,000 young people at a camp for disadvantaged kids. He served as principal of a Christian school. He graduated from Gordon Conwell Theological Seminary in 2000, loaded up the family, and headed for the mission field in southern Mexico where he pioneered a ministry called El Monte... but that's another story!

Today, Ed is a missionary with WEC International, serving on staff at CIT, a missionary training center that is sending workers around the world. He and Debbie enjoy their many grandchildren and wonder what the future holds for them.

Ed Somerville and his Mom

Made in the USA
Columbia, SC
10 October 2020

22553418R00124